The Happy Hollisters

and the

Merry-Go-Round Mystery

BY JERRY WEST

Illustrated by Helen S. Hamilton

GARDEN CITY, N.Y.

Doubleday & Company, Inc.

Printed in the United States of America

Contents

CHAPTER 1

Exciting Plans

"I'LL bet I can swing higher'n you!" Ricky Hollister cried as he raced toward the swings in the schoolyard.

"No, you can't," Holly answered, running alongside her red-haired, seven-year-old brother.

Holly, known as a tomboy, was only a year younger than the freckle-nosed lad. Her brown pigtails flew out over her shoulders as she ran. The two children reached the swings at the same moment and plopped into seats.

It was a lovely April morning. A soft spring rain had fallen the night before, covering the schoolyard with puddles. Hopping over one after another of them came the children's brother and sister, Pete and Pam Hollister.

"Hi! Want a push?" Pete called out. He was a good-looking boy of twelve with a blond crew cut.

"Yes," Ricky and Holly chorused.

Pete gave Ricky a hard shove, while Pam, a slender, golden-haired girl of ten with a sweet smile, sent her sister soaring.

"Who's winning?" Ricky called.

"Okay, that's high enough. We have a good start," Ricky shouted.

Holly grinned impishly and pumped hard. Higher and higher went the children.

"Who's winning?" Ricky called to a group of schoolmates who had gathered to watch.

"It's a tie," replied plump, brown-eyed Donna Martin, showing her dimples. She was in Holly's class and lived near the Hollisters. "You Hollisters always have so much fun together."

"That's why we call ourselves the Happy Hollisters," Pam said, smiling. "But Donna's right, Ricky. You and Holly are neck and neck."

"Anyhow, I can do something Holly can't," Ricky said.

"What's that?"

6

"Jump off the swing while it's still going."

"Please don't. You might hurt yourself," Holly pleaded. "Besides, there's a big puddle in front of your swing."

Ricky looked down at the water and said, "Oh, I can jump right over that. Watch me!"

As his swing went forward again, the boy let go and sailed through the air.

Plop! He landed in the center of the puddle, splashing his trousers with muddy water up to the knees. As Holly and the others laughed, Pam said kindly, "You'd better hurry home and change to dry pants, Rick. You'll still have time before the bell."

Ricky raced off but returned just as the principal's voice boomed over the loud-speaker, located above the main entrance of Lincoln School.

"Attention, please!" Mr. Russell ordered. "All pupils are to go directly to the auditorium when the first bell rings this morning. We will hold our assembly earlier today to discuss more plans for the coming school fair."

Just then the bell rang. Everyone hurried toward the large assembly hall.

"This year the money we earn is going to the Shoreham Day Nursery," Pam said to Holly as they hustled toward their assigned seats.

"The place where we've seen those cute little children?" Holly asked, and Pam nodded.

Soon everyone was seated quietly in the big auditorium. Mr. Russell crossed the stage and led the children and their teachers in pledging allegiance to the flag and singing "The Star-Spangled Banner." Then he said, "Plans are coming along nicely for our school fair which, as you know, will be held for three days next month. Several committees have been formed and chairmen appointed. But we still need a few more events for the fair. If you have any suggestions, will you please rise and I'll call on you one at a time."

Instantly a young boy arose. The Hollisters recognized him as Jeff Hunter, a friend of Ricky's.

"Yes, Jeff?" the principal said.

"Could we have a merry-go-round this year?" Jeff asked.

"That's an idea," Mr. Russell replied. "How many others would like a merry-go-round?"

Almost everyone raised his hand and the auditorium was filled with murmurs of approval.

"I'm sure we could raise a lot of money with one," said Mr. Russell. "But a merry-go-round might be hard to find. Who will volunteer to locate one?"

Pete Hollister stood up. "I will, sir."

As Pete sat down his classmate Joey Brill jumped up. Joey was a bully who had given the Hollisters a hard time ever since they had moved to Shoreham the year before.

"Mr. Russell," he said, "let's change the date of our fair. The Jumbo Carnival is on the same days and I'd like my old job back."

Joey had been a ticket taker for the merry-go-round

at the carnival the year before until the carrousel had broken down.

"I'm afraid we can't change the date," Mr. Russell replied. "And we will have a merry-go-round—that is, if Pete Hollister can find one."

When Joey realized that he had failed in his selfish plea, he scowled and sat down hard in his seat. He slumped low in his chair and made a face at the principal, though Mr. Russell could not see him, and whispered, "Pete Hollister's a big know-it-all!"

With that he reached over and slapped Pete on the back of the head.

Mr. Russell saw this and called out, "Joey Brill, leave the assembly at once and go to my office."

Joey rose from his seat, pushed roughly past the other children in his row, and stomped out of the auditorium.

The principal then asked if there were any more ideas for the school fair and Dave Mead stood up. He was Pete's best friend.

"We older boys had a soap-box derby at last year's fair. How about a derby for the younger boys this year?" he suggested.

Everybody in the lower grades cheered when they heard this, and the principal agreed that it was a fine idea.

"Would you be the chairman, Dave?" Mr. Russell asked, and Dave said he would be glad to.

Ann Hunter thought it would be nice to have a committee make rag dolls and other yarn and cloth

Joey stomped out of the auditorium.

toys to be sold at the fair. "I'd like to nominate Pam Hollister for chairman," she said.

Pam, beaming, accepted and began to think about selecting her committee. Just then Holly Hollister hopped up out of her seat. "Oh, I have a suggestion," she cried out. "I'd like to give donkey-cart rides using our burro, Domingo."

The gleeful smiles that followed her remark showed that Holly's suggestion would be a popular event at the fair.

After assembly was over, the children went back to their classrooms, but it was hard to concentrate on studies for the rest of the day. When school was dismissed that afternoon, Ricky raced up to Dave Mead and said breathlessly: "I want to get into the soap-box derby. Please, may I?"

"Why, sure," Dave said. "The more the merrier."

"Oh, good," Ricky said, and hurried toward home to figure out a way to build a midget car.

Holly arrived home soon after her brother and went directly to the garage where Domingo was kept. The garage was located in the big back yard of the Hollister home, situated on beautiful Pine Lake. The house was old-fashioned and rambling, a very comfortable dwelling for Mr. and Mrs. Hollister and their five children.

All the children except Sue, a dark-haired, four-year-old, went to school. The little girl saw her sister running toward the garage and hurried up to her.

"Oh, Sue!" Holly exclaimed. "I'm going to give

"Whoa!" Holly ordered.

donkey rides at the school fair. Let's practice right now. I'll hitch up the cart and you can ride with me."

She opened the garage door and went to a stall where Domingo was standing quietly. Nearby was a small, two-wheel wooden cart. Soon Holly and Sue had the burro harnessed to it.

"Okay, Sue. Hop in," Holly said. When the two girls were seated, she called out, "Giddap, Domingo!"

The burro seemed to like the idea of taking his two youngest mistresses for a ride. But instead of jogging along slowly, the way he usually did, Domingo trotted very fast.

"Whee!" Holly shouted. She drove the burro clear around the house, then along the driveway.

"I'll turn back to the garage now," the girl told

herself. When she pulled on the left rein, the donkey turned very quickly. "Whoa!" Holly ordered. "Not so fast, Domingo!"

But the two-wheel cart already had tilted over on one wheel.

Out tumbled the two girls!

CHAPTER 2

Sue, "Look Out!"

AFTER tumbling head over heels out of the donkey cart, Sue and Holly rolled over and over on the ground. Domingo ran on for a short distance, then stopped, nervously twitching his ears.

Holly was the first to pick herself up. "Are you all right, Sue?" she asked.

"I—I guess I am," the little girl replied, catching her breath. Then she added, "Holly, was that an act we're going to put on for the children at the school fair?"

"An act?" Holly asked, then she laughed. "Oh no, Sue, that was an accident."

The two girls brushed themselves off, then hurried over to the burro.

"Domingo," said Sue, shaking her finger, "please don't do that again." The donkey hung his head.

At that moment Pete Hollister hurried up the

15

driveway, righted the overturned cart, and said, "I just heard where we can get a merry-go-round!"

"Where?" asked Ricky, running out of the garage.

"Jimmy Cox told me that a man named Mr. Day has one. He lives right here in town."

"Yikes!" Ricky exclaimed. "Let's you and I go see him right away."

The two boys set off on a run. In ten minutes they were in front of Mr. Day's house.

"Jiminy, I don't see any merry-go-round here," Ricky said.

"Maybe Mr. Day stores it somewhere else," Pete said hopefully, as they knocked on the door. It was opened by a friendly-looking little man who invited the boys inside.

After Pete introduced himself and his brother, he said, "We understand you have a merry-go-round, Mr. Day."

"Oh yes, I have," the man replied. "I made it myself, and I'm very proud of it."

Quickly Pete explained that they needed one for their school fair.

"Oh, I think you'd like mine," the man said. "Come, I'll show it to you. It's in the basement."

He led the boys downstairs.

"Yikes! How will we ever get it out of the basement?" Ricky asked.

"No trouble at all," the man said. "Look! There it is over there. Isn't it a beauty?"

"Domingo, don't do that again!"

He pointed to a workbench in the far corner on which stood a tiny carrousel.

"Oh, it's a miniature," Pete said, and told Mr. Day they were looking for a merry-go-round on which children could ride.

"Sorry I can't oblige you," the man said, "but if you can use my little carrousel in any way, you're welcome to it."

He walked over to the bench and pressed a button on the side of the toy. Instantly it started to turn round and round. At the same time a little music box piped a gay tune.

"This is great!" Pete said. "Maybe we could put it in my dad's store window to advertise the school fair."

Mr. Hollister ran a combination hardware, toy, and sporting goods shop in the center of Shoreham. It was called The Trading Post.

"You're welcome to it, son," Mr. Day said. He put the little merry-go-round in a strong wooden carton. "Can you fellows carry this between you?"

"Sure," Pete replied. "And we'll be very careful. We'll bring it back when the fair is over, Mr. Day. Thank you very much."

Arriving at The Trading Post, the boys showed the little merry-go-round to their father. The tall, dark-haired man's brown eyes twinkled.

"That will be a fine display for our window," he said.

Pete quickly cleared one of the show windows

to make room for the carrousel and set the toy in motion. Before long a crowd of people gathered outside the store to admire the display. A few minutes later, Pete put a sign alongside the merry-go-round which read:

COME RIDE THE MERRY-GO-ROUND
NEXT MONTH
AT THE LINCOLN SCHOOL FAIR

Ricky was standing on the sidewalk beside a stout man when suddenly he heard Joey Brill's voice. The bully was talking to Will Wilson, his best friend, who got into nearly as much trouble as Joey did.

"That's a fake ad," Joey said. "Pete Hollister won't be able to find a big merry-go-round. If the owner of the Jumbo Carnival can't locate one, how can Pete?"

Ricky said nothing but went back into the store to tell his brother and Mr. Hollister.

"I imagine merry-go-rounds are hard to find," Mr. Hollister admitted. "I hope you haven't taken on an impossible job, Pete."

"Don't worry, Dad," Pete said. "I'm sure we can get one for the fair."

Ricky then told his father he had looked all over the Hollister cellar and garage but could not find any axles or wheels with which to start his soap-box derby racer.

"I'll have to use real good ones if I want to make a speedy car, Dad," he said.

Mr. Hollister put an arm around his young son. "I'll make a bargain with you, Ricky. I have a set of fine axles and wheels here. I'll give them to you in return for helping me."

"Swell!" Ricky exclaimed, jumping up and down.

His father led him to the hardware department and gave him four shiny metal wheels and two stout axles.

"Gee, thanks, Dad!" Ricky exclaimed, and ran off toward home with the car parts.

He went directly to his father's workbench in the cellar. Finding a saw, some nails and screws, a hammer and a screwdriver, Ricky set about making a wooden frame on which to attach the axles.

Half an hour later, Jeff Hunter ran down the cellar steps. "Whizzigers, you've really got a lot done on your racer," he said, as Ricky finished attaching the wheels.

"Let's try it out, Jeff," Ricky said proudly.

The two boys carried the frame into the yard. They placed a board across the center, then Jeff sat on it and Ricky pushed him to the driveway.

"We'll make believe this is the race track," Ricky said. "Hold on tight!"

He put his hands on Jeff's shoulders and pushed as hard as he could.

"Wow! This is really speedy!" Jeff cried. Then suddenly he shouted in alarm, "Sue, look out!"

The little girl was pushing her doll carriage from the lawn onto the driveway just ahead of him. Ricky had not yet made a steering wheel for his racer, so Jeff could not turn. And Sue was so close there was not time for him to drag his feet to stop the car.

Crash! It hit the carriage, knocking Sue's doll high into the air. As it fell to the ground, the little girl wailed, "Oh, my baby's hurt-ed! Look! A piece of her head's broke off! Quick! Somebody take her to a doll hospital!" Tears ran down Sue's cheeks.

Pam hurried from the house to see what the trouble was. "Don't worry, Sue," she said. "I'll glue your dolly's head together. And after this you'd better take your unbreakable dolls out riding."

"I'm awfully sorry," Ricky said.

"Me, too," Jeff added. Then he suggested, "Ricky, you'd better get a steering wheel made for this right away."

As the boys carried the frame of the racer back to the cellar, Pam took Sue's doll into the house for repairs. In no time at all it was mended and Sue was happy again.

Just before dinnertime, Pete ran into the house very much excited. "I just found out something about the Jumbo Carnival," he told his brothers and sisters.

Pete explained that he had been talking to Officer Cal, a nice policeman who had helped the Hollisters solve several mysteries.

"Cal said the Shoreham officials don't want the Jumbo Carnival in town," the boy said. "The carnival people left last year without cleaning up the fairgrounds and the town had to."

"Then the carnival won't be held here at all?" Pam asked gleefully.

"Not inside the town limits, anyway," Pete replied. "But it'll be just outside Shoreham. I learned, too, that the carnival is owned by a Zack Byrd and his partner Tom Weel. And, as Joey said, they're still looking for a merry-go-round to replace their broken-down one!"

After supper, while the older children were doing their homework, Sue went to her mother and said, "I'd like to do something for the school fair, too."

"What would you like to do?" asked Mrs. Hollister, a slender, pretty woman with wavy blond hair.

"Maybe I could be a gypsy fortuneteller."

"Wow! This is really speedy!"

"I think we might arrange that," her mother replied, smiling. "Come with me, dear."

She led Sue to the attic, where costumes were stored. In a few minutes, Sue and Mrs. Hollister were back downstairs with Sue dressed as a gypsy.

"And look what we found, Daddy," the little girl said to her father, holding up a small round fish bowl.

"Why, it's a crystal ball," Mr. Hollister remarked, putting down his newspaper.

"I'll show you how the gypsies work it, Daddy," Sue said excitedly.

She set the bowl upside down on the coffee table and covered it with a black cloth. Then she whisked off the cloth, put her hands on the bowl, and gazed into it.

"What do you see?" Mrs. Hollister asked.

She thought for a long time, then said, "Lollipops and ice-cream sodas."

"Who's eating them?" Mrs. Hollister smiled.

"Why, I am," Sue said, giggling.

Ricky, who was in the next room supposedly studying his spelling, came out when he heard his parents laughing. Spying the gypsy's fish bowl, a twinkle came into his eyes.

Sue, meanwhile, had gone to the other side of the room and climbed up to her daddy's lap to listen to her nightly bedtime story. When it was over and Mrs. Hollister was leading her small daughter out of the room toward the stairs, Sue remembered her crystal ball.

"Wait a minute, Mommy. I forgot something," she cried, rushing over to the fish bowl. As she reached for it, Sue let out a cry.

"Mommy, Mommy, it's magical! Look!"

Mrs. Hollister hurried to her daughter's side and looked down into the fish bowl. Sure enough! There inside was a circus clown standing on his head.

Suddenly Sue and her parents heard a squeal of delight. Looking in the direction of the sound, they saw Ricky, hiding behind a chair, his hand over his mouth in an effort to hide his glee.

"Oh, Ricky, you played a trick on me," Sue cried, picking up the fish bowl and looking inside. "You pasted a picture in my crystal ball."

Ricky ran off laughing just as the telephone rang. Mr. Hollister answered it.

"I'll show you how the gypsies work."

"Hello," he said. "A telegram, you say. Yes, will you read it to me, please?"

After a short pause, Sue, excited, cried out, "Is it something important?"

Mr. Hollister hung up, smiling. "Something you'll like. Your uncle Russ is coming here tomorrow afternoon. He's bringing some visitors with him."

"Who are they?"

"I don't know. It's a surprise."

CHAPTER 3

A Tricky Roof

THE Hollister children tried to guess who the visitors might be that were coming with their uncle Russ. They loved their humorous uncle, who was Mr. Hollister's younger brother. He was a cartoonist whose funnies appeared in the daily newspapers.

"Maybe the surprise is Aunt Marge and our cousins Jean and Teddy," Holly suggested.

"Yikes! I hope so!" Ricky yelled.

The children always liked to have the Hollisters from Crestwood visit them, and moreover Aunt Marge usually brought some homemade candy with her!

"Well, we'll have to wait until tomorrow to find out," Mrs. Hollister said.

The children sighed but were happy at the thought that the next day would be Friday and that meant a weekend of good times ahead of them. Immediately after school the next afternoon Pam and Holly hurried home and went straight to their mother.

"What a nice place!" Sue remarked.

"We'd like to visit the Shoreham Day Nursery,"
Pam said to her, "and talk to Mrs. Griffith, the
director, about our school fair. You know, all the
money from it is going to the nursery."

"That's splendid," said Mrs. Hollister, and gave
permission for the girls to go.

Sue pleaded to walk with them and soon the
three children were on their way. The Shoreham
Day Nursery was a large oblong-shaped house which
had been converted into a nursery for young children
of Shoreham whose mothers worked. The youngsters
were brought to the nursery early in the morning and
picked up in the late afternoon.

The girls climbed the front steps and Pam knocked
on the door. Mrs. Griffith, a kindly, middle-aged

woman, opened it. After Pam introduced herself and her sisters, Mrs. Griffith said, "Please come in. We love to have visitors. And I'm sure you would like to see our children."

"Yes, we would," Holly answered.

After the Hollister girls had taken off their jackets, Pam and Mrs. Griffith discussed how the proceeds of this year's Lincoln School Fair would be used.

"We are so delighted!" Mrs. Griffith exclaimed. "We do need a lot of things. Come, I'll take you on a tour."

To the left side of the hallway was a room with small-size tables and chairs. Children from two to six years of age were seated at them, finger-painting, coloring, and playing games. Directly in back of the playroom was the dining room and off of it a white, sparkling kitchen.

"What a nice place for the children to stay while their mommies are working," Sue remarked.

"We have bedrooms upstairs which I think you would like to see," Mrs. Griffith said, leading the way up a flight of steps.

The entire second floor was taken up with small bedrooms. In some were cribs with high sides for the younger children. The other rooms contained rows of low cots.

"Our children take two-hour naps every afternoon," Mrs. Griffith said. Then she pointed to a crib in a far corner. "This afternoon everyone's up but Tommy. He's a real sleepyhead."

As she spoke a two-year-old boy sat up in the crib and began rubbing his eyes.

"Tommy plays so hard," the woman said, "that he sleeps longer than the others."

The little fellow did not say a word, but stood up in the crib, grabbed one side of it, and shook the bars hard.

Rattle, rattle, rattle!

"Just a minute, Tommy!" Mrs. Griffith laughed. "You'll break that!"

But the small boy was eager to be up and playing. So he rattled the crib even harder.

Bang!

The side fell off and clattered to the floor. The little boy lost his balance for a moment, then sat down *kerplunk* on the mattress.

"Oh dear!" the director exclaimed in despair. "These cribs are so old they're ready to fall apart. It's a wonder to me that one of the children hasn't fallen out and hurt himself long before this."

"Can't we take him downstairs and play with him?" Pam asked.

Mrs. Griffith carried Tommy to the first floor. The little boy sat down at one of the tables and began to play with some large building blocks.

"I'll help you," Sue offered. She pulled up a little chair and sat down beside him.

Together they made a bridge and Mrs. Griffith marveled at how skillful Sue Hollister was. She could actually make the curved blocks stay together in an arch.

"Is there anything I can do to help?" Pam asked.

"Why, yes, there is," Mrs. Griffith replied. "These little folks must wash their hands and faces before their mothers call for them. Will you see that they do it?"

"I'll be glad to," Pam replied.

As Pam led a little girl from the room, Holly spied some children playing in the back yard. Receiving permission to go out with them, she put on her jacket and skipped outside.

"What a wonderful playground!" she thought.

There were monkey bars, a sandbox, swings, and a sliding board. But best of all was the playhouse, a one-story wooden building large enough to allow three or four children to play inside comfortably. At the moment a girl and a boy about five years old were playing house inside it. Holly poked her head in and looked around.

"Come play house with us," the little girl said with a smile. "We're the Byrd twins. I'm Jill and he's Jack."

Holly introduced herself and joined in their game. They were setting a table with gaily decorated aluminum dishes.

"It's time for the tea party," said Jill.

"I don't like tea," Jack spoke up. "I want a big chocolate ice-cream soda."

31

"Here's one," said Holly, giggling, and filled a cup with some dirt from the floor. She topped it off with a handful of white pebbles.

Jack made a face. "I mean real," he said.

"Maybe Mommy will get us each one tonight," Jill said hopefully.

"No, she won't have any money for that," her twin answered soberly.

The three children had a pretend meal. Holly soon grew tired of this, however, as talk of ice cream had made her hungry. She decided to go outside and look at the playhouse. What an interesting house it was!

"It's not much taller than Daddy," Holly said to herself. "I'll bet I could climb up on the roof real easy."

"Help! Help!" Holly cried.

She went outside and stepped onto a window sill. By standing on her tiptoes she could reach the edge of the roof. The little tomboy pulled herself up and soon was astride the peaked roof.

"Oh, this is fun," she thought, looking down on several youngsters who were playing in a big sandbox below.

Holly had always wanted to walk on top of a house. This was her chance. Step by step she went carefully along the peak of the roof, shading her eyes with one hand and scanning the countryside. Holly was imagining herself to be a sailor, high atop the crow's-nest of a great clipper ship.

Suddenly her foot slipped.

"Oops!" Holly exclaimed.

She sat down hard on the roof, digging her heels against the slope to keep from sliding farther. But her shoes would not grip the slippery shingles of the roof. Closer to the edge she slid.

Holly was just about to tumble off when the belt of her jacket caught on a nail protruding from the roof's edge. Dangling in midair, she cried out, "Help! Help!"

Jack and Jill ran from the little house and looked up at her.

"Oh!" they cried in alarm, and Jack added, "I'll go call Mrs. Griffith."

He dashed into the house and in a few seconds the director appeared, with Pam and Sue at her heels.

"Gracious, child!" the woman exclaimed.

"Could that be Uncle Russ?"

She ran to the playhouse and caught Holly in her arms just as the belt gave way. Pam and Sue gasped in relief.

"Oh, thank you!" Holly said. "I won't do it again. I promise."

She returned to the nursery with Pam and Mrs. Griffith. Pam asked the director what she would like most to get for the nursery from the money raised at the school fair.

"I believe new cots and cribs," she said.

About this time Mrs. Byrd arrived to take her children home. She was a pretty woman with dark hair, but her eyes were sad. After she had left with Jack and Jill, Pam asked Mrs. Griffith about the young woman's sad expression.

"Mrs. Byrd is a widow," the director told her. "The twins' father died a few years ago and their mother has had to work ever since to support Jack and Jill. She doesn't earn a great deal, though, because she isn't very strong. It's hard for her."

Pam felt very sorry for Mrs. Byrd. As she was thinking about this, Holly suddenly said, "We'd better go home. Remember, Uncle Russ is coming and bringing surprise visitors."

The girls thanked Mrs. Griffith for showing them the nursery and Pam said she would like to come the next day and help.

"Fine. I'll expect you around noon."

When the girls arrived home, they found Pete and Ricky at the curb waiting for Uncle Russ.

Just then the children heard the sound of a plane. Glancing up, they saw a pontoon plane circling above their house.

"That pilot's flying low," Pam said, looking up. "I wonder if he knows us."

"He seems to," Pete answered. "Look, he's wig-wagging the wings of the plane!"

"Yikes!" Ricky shouted. "Do you suppose that could be Uncle Russ and he's not coming by car after all?"

The plane circled lower and lower and finally began a long glide down toward the lake.

"Jeepers, it's going to land right near our dock!" Pete exclaimed.

The children dashed across the lawn toward the waterfront to meet it.

CHAPTER 4

Strange Movies

As THE Hollister children stood on the dock they could see the plane gently touch down upon the lake and start to taxi toward them. The plane was a large one—for six or eight passengers—with a door in the side of the fuselage.

At the same time, Mr. Hollister drove his station wagon into the driveway. He quickly hopped out and ran toward the waterfront. Mrs. Hollister, seeing the excitement from a window, hurried from the house to join her family.

As the approaching plane came close to the dock, the pilot turned off the motor. Just then the door opened and a happy-looking man poked his head out.

"Uncle Russ! Uncle Russ!" the children screamed. He was tall, slender, and resembled the children's father, but was several years younger.

"Well, here I am!" he called out, waving cheerily.

"Who are the other visitors?" Ricky asked excitedly, as one of the pontoons touched the side of the dock.

"I'll let you know as soon as you tie our plane with this rope," Uncle Russ said with a grin.

He tossed a coil to Pete and the boy snubbed it onto a dock post.

"Well, now, here are your visitors," Uncle Russ said, and beckoned to two people inside the plane to step out.

The children held their breaths and Holly said, "Oh, I just can't wait to see who they are."

Out of the door of the plane stepped Gram and Gramp Hollister! The family cried out gleefully and flung their arms about the elderly couple. Gramp was a lean, rugged-looking man with twinkling eyes. Gram, a bit plump, had a lovely smile.

"What a wonderful surprise this is!" Mrs. Hollister said, kissing Gram.

Gramp shook the hand of his son John, saying, "I'll bet you didn't expect to see us."

He explained that they had been staying with Uncle Russ's family in Crestwood and decided to make the surprise visit.

In a moment the pilot of the plane appeared at the door. He was a stocky man in a black leather jacket. Uncle Russ introduced him as Al Jordan.

"Al and I are old friends," he explained, "and he offered to take me for a ride while I made some sketches for a new comic strip which I'm drawing about a young pilot."

Gramp's eyes sparkled as he said, "Wait until you see some of them."

"Oh, let's see them right away," Ricky begged.

The other children clamored for them also, so

Out stepped Gram and Gramp.

Uncle Russ took several out of his case and showed them.

"Boy," said Pete, looking at an unfinished story, "that'll be nifty. The pilot even went to the moon but he didn't stop there. Why?"

"Good reason," Ricky chuckled. "The man in the moon wasn't home!"

There were laughs and groans at Ricky's joke, then the children took the visitors' arms and started toward the house.

Gram and Gramp Hollister lived in the town of Froston in Canada. They had moved there after Gramp's retirement and had bought Snowflake Camp, a group of cabins for winter vacationists. The children had had a wonderful adventure while visiting there on Thanksgiving.

"Boys," Mr. Hollister called, "help with this luggage," and his sons returned.

The pilot handed out several suitcases from the baggage compartment. Then the happy group headed for the house and got ready for supper. Mrs. Hollister had prepared enough for the extra guests. Pam and Ricky quickly put another leaf in the dining-room table and soon everyone was seated around it.

Almost immediately the children began to talk about the coming school fair and the parts they would have in helping to make it a success.

"Please visit us long enough to see the fair," Holly begged, and said it was only three weeks off.

Uncle Russ and the pilot said they would try to return. Gram and Gramp looked at each other and, with a wink at Sue, Gramp said to her, "Do you think you could put up with us for that long?"

"We want you to stay here always," Sue chirped, and the other children said they did too.

When Pam told about what her committee was making for the fair, Gram offered to help her with the yarn and cloth toys.

"I remember an old rag doll pattern we used when I was a little girl," Gram said. "We stuffed them with cotton, painted on sweet faces, and added different-colored yarn for hair."

Gramp said he would like to assist too, but not with rag dolls!

"Could you help me make my auto racer?" Ricky asked.

"Of course," Gramp replied. "We'll trim it up so fancy it will look like next year's car."

After the children had cleared away the supper dishes and had stacked them in the washer, Gramp said, "I have some movies to show you which I took on your last visit to Froston. Would you like to see them now?"

"Oh, let's!" Ricky shouted.

"Please!" the others cried.

"I hope you won't be too disappointed in them," Gram said seriously. "They turned out mighty queer."

"But, Gramp, you're very good at taking movies," Pam said. "What's wrong with them?"

Gram smiled and said maybe the children could guess. They all sat down in the living room and Pete hurried to get the movie screen from the hall closet. Ricky set up the moving-picture projector.

Gramp, meanwhile, had gone upstairs to bring the film from his suitcase. It was threaded into the projector and when everything was ready Mrs. Hollister turned out the lights.

Gramp switched on the machine and everyone stared excitedly at the screen. There were Pete, Pam, Ricky, Sue, and Holly riding on a dog sled. But the dogs were not running forward. They were backing up!

"Yikes, we're funny!" Ricky cried out, and everyone chuckled.

The next scene showed a ski jump with a skier

at the bottom. Suddenly he began to flap his arms and fly through the air backward to the top of the jump.

As the children laughed, Gramp said, "You see what I mean? I must have been holding my camera backward when I took these pictures."

"Oh, you're an old tease," Pam said.

Next came a picture of the Hollister children throwing snowballs. How funny it looked! The snowballs came right out of the air and landed in the children's mittens.

Everyone in the room was laughing loudly as the reel ended, and Pete said, "Now, Gramp, please run them the right way."

The kindly gentleman chuckled and promised to do this at once. When they were finished, and Mr. Hollister and Pete were putting away the screen and projector, Ricky said, "You know what would be nice? A ride in Mr. Jordan's plane."

The pilot looked out the window, then back at the Hollisters. "It's still light enough to take you children on a short flight if your parents will allow it."

"Oh, boy!"

"Please, Mother!"

"Please, Dad!"

"All right," Mrs. Hollister nodded, and there was a whoop of glee.

Putting on their jackets, they hurried outside with the pilot and ran to the dock, with the grownups

Ricky set up the motion-picture projector.

following at a walk. Mr. Jordan opened the door and he and the children piled in. Mr. Hollister untied the rope which held the plane to the dock and tossed it to Pete. Then the door was closed and locked. Pete sat alongside the pilot with the other children behind them.

"All set?" Mr. Jordan asked, turning around and smiling.

"Okay," they replied.

He pressed the starter button. The children waved out the window to their parents as the plane taxied out onto Pine Lake.

"Here we go!" Mr. Jordan said, giving his ship the gun.

The pontoons skimmed over the surface of the

water. Then like magic, the plane was lifted into the air.

"Hurray, we're flying!" Holly shouted.

The sun had already set and the lake seemed like a big looking glass below them. Several motorboats crisscrossed the surface like tiny darts.

"Let's make believe they're submarines," Ricky said, "and we're going to bomb them."

The boy peered through the window and then grabbed an imaginary handle. He jerked it and cried, "Bombs away!"

Holly giggled and said, "Your nothing-bomb landed right on a submarine, Ricky!"

"I think we'd better land now before it gets too dark," Mr. Jordan said to Pete. He nosed the plane down in a long glide. As they dropped lower and lower, Pete saw a motorboat zigzagging toward them.

"What's wrong with those two boys in that boat?" he cried. "They're right in our path."

"I can't understand it," Mr. Jordan declared. "They can certainly hear us. I'll give them the standard warning that we're going to land."

The pilot wigwagged the plane's wings a few times. Finally the motorboat veered off and headed across the lake.

"Whew!" Pete exclaimed. "Guess it's all clear now."

The pilot nodded and brought the plane lower in a steep glide.

Pete's eyes were still following the motorboat. Suddenly he stiffened and yelled, "Hey! That boat has turned around and it's heading into our path. Crickets! We're going to land right on top of them!"

CHAPTER 5

Zip Is Worried

WHEN the pilot realized that the plane could not land without hitting the boys in the motorboat, he gunned the engine. The plane soared into the sky.

"Wow! That was a close one!" Pete whistled.

"I've never seen anyone so reckless as those kids," Al Jordan declared angrily. "Don't they have any sense?"

The narrow escape must have frightened the boys in the boat because they roared off and left plenty of room for the pontoon plane to come down. Mr. Jordan circled the spot again, then landed.

Once more the motorboat came toward them. In it were Joey Brill and Will Wilson! As the boys drew close, the pilot slid back a little window in the cockpit and began to scold Will and Joey.

"Didn't you see me trying to land?" he said severely. "You might have been badly hurt if the pontoons had hit you."

Instead of apologizing, the boys looked defiant.

"The Hollisters don't own this lake," Joey bellowed. "We can go where we please."

47

"You have no right to endanger your own lives or anybody else's," Al said. "Now go along."

Joey started to say something but evidently thought better of it. He kept still and the two boys sped off in their boat.

Al Jordan taxied the plane up to the dock. After everyone was out, the pilot and Pete tied it securely to the dock. Then they went inside the house.

While the younger children were preparing for bed, Pete and Pam talked to Uncle Russ in the living room about their search for a merry-go-round. "Have you ever seen one in your part of the country that we might borrow?" Pete asked.

His uncle thought for a minute, then snapped his fingers. "There's a man right in Crestwood who owns two merry-go-rounds," he said. "A large one

"The Hollisters don't own this lake!" Joey cried.

and a small one. His name is Mr. De Marco."

As Pete and Pam listened excitedly, Uncle Russ told them that the small carrousel for little children to ride on was mounted on a flat trailer to be pulled by a car. The large merry-go-round, which could be knocked down in sections for easy transportation, was carried on Mr. De Marco's truck.

"Mr. De Marco hasn't used the carrousels recently," the cartoonist said, "because he's been ill."

"Then perhaps we could borrow them for the school fair!" Pam said.

"Or anyway rent them," Pete added.

Just then Mrs. Hollister came down from the second floor. She had just kissed Sue, Holly, and Ricky good night. When she heard the exciting news about merry-go-rounds in Crestwood, she too was thrilled.

"Suppose you write to Mr. De Marco," Mrs. Hollister suggested, "and ask him about his merry-go-rounds."

"Oh, gee, Mother," Pete said, "I want to find out right away. Please, may I call him by long distance."

"All right, dear."

Pete was in such a hurry that he tripped on the rug and knocked the phone to the floor. He picked it up and soon was talking to Mr. De Marco in Crestwood.

Pete explained all about the school fair in Shoreham. After talking for a few minutes his face brightened.

Boy and dog circled the house twice.

"You would, really?" the boy said excitedly. "When may we come and get them? You prefer that we come right away? Well, I'll have to talk to my parents about it."

There was a slight pause, then Pete continued, "Oh, thank you, Mr. De Marco," he said, and hung up.

"Tell us everything," Pam demanded.

Pete grinned. "We may use both his merry-go-rounds *free* because it's for charity. And he wants us to get them right away. Mr. De Marco won't be well enough to use them for at least another month."

"Oh, Uncle Russ, isn't this exciting?" Pam said.

Mr. Hollister came into the room and was told what Pete had learned.

"When may we get the merry-go-rounds?" Pam asked.

Before her father had time to answer, Zip, the Hollisters' beautiful golden collie dog, dashed into the room, and, barking excitedly, ran to one of the windows. By now it was dark outside.

"What's the matter, Zip?" Pete asked, going to the window.

He peered outside but could see nobody. Zip continued to bark. "Do you suppose there's a prowler out there?" Mrs. Hollister asked.

Pete volunteered to look. Putting on a jacket, he took his father's flashlight and went outside with Zip bounding at his heels. Boy and dog circled the house twice but could find no one.

"Maybe it was just a cat or a rabbit," Pete thought as they returned to the house.

"Who was it?" Mrs. Hollister asked.

"We couldn't find anyone," Pete replied, patting Zip.

The others were discussing how the Hollisters might get the two merry-go-rounds from Crestwood.

"Perhaps some men over there could drive them here," Pam suggested.

"I think I have a better idea," Pete said enthusiastically. "Why don't we go to Crestwood and pick them up?"

"But Crestwood is an overnight trip by car," said Mr. Hollister. "I couldn't take so much time from business and besides, you children mustn't miss school."

"Maybe we could miss two days," said Pete. "It's for a good cause. Why can't we all fly to Crestwood with Uncle Russ tomorrow and bring the merry-go-rounds back with us? Could we, Mr. Jordan?"

The pilot smiled. "I'd like to but I'm afraid my plane wouldn't hold everybody. That would be four adults, including Gram and Gramp, plus five children, your uncle Russ and me. Eleven people, all together," he said.

"Count Gramp and me out," Gram said. "I've had enough plane riding for a while."

After a discussion it was decided that Sue would stay at home with her grandparents. The rest of the family would fly to Crestwood on Saturday afternoon.

Pete's light beamed over the water.

They would stay at Uncle Russ's home two nights and start back with the merry-go-rounds Monday morning.

"There's just one problem," Pete said. "We'll need a car to haul the small merry-go-round to Shoreham."

"I can settle that right now," said Uncle Russ. "You can borrow mine and I'll pick it up next time I'm around here."

Al Jordan said he would be flying the cartoonist again soon. "I'll drop him off here."

Pam chuckled. "Oh, please don't. Uncle Russ might hurt himself." Then she added seriously, "Won't it be exciting to ride home with a merry-go-round? Mother can drive the car and Dad the truck!"

"And won't it be fun to stay overnight with your cousins Teddy and Jean?" Mrs. Hollister said. "I'll phone their mother."

"And see all our old friends in Crestwood," Pete added.

While Mr. and Mrs. Hollister took Gram and Gramp, Uncle Russ, and Mr. Jordan to the guest rooms, Pete and Pam stood in the second-floor hall discussing the plane trip. Suddenly they heard Zip bark again downstairs. He was bounding from one window to another.

"There's somebody outside, I'm sure," Pete said. "I'm going to look again."

"I'll go with you," Pam volunteered.

Pete grabbed a flashlight from the drawer in the hall table and together the children dashed outdoors with the dog. The light was flashed among the bushes around the house. But not even a rabbit was in sight.

Pete and Pam went all the way to the dock where the pontoon plane had been moored for the night. Still they saw no one. Zip sniffed around the dock for a minute, then waded into the water.

"What do you see, old boy?" Pete asked.

Both children remained perfectly quiet. Pete beamed the light over the still water but nothing unusual was to be seen.

"Come on, boy, let's go back into the house."

Zip waded out of the water and shook a shower of drops from his thick coat. Then he followed the boy and his sister inside.

The next morning Pete was the first of the children to reach the kitchen where his mother was preparing breakfast. After she had kissed him, Mrs. Hollister said, "Pete, will you bring in the milk from the back porch?"

The boy opened the door and cried, "Mr. Jordan's airplane! It's gone!"

CHAPTER 6

The Search

When Pete discovered that the plane was gone, he cried out in alarm and ran into the house to tell the others.

"My plane is gone?" Al Jordan asked in disbelief, as he hurried downstairs and ran outside with Pete.

All the Hollisters followed to the dock where the plane had been tied the night before.

"Do you suppose somebody stole it?" Ricky asked.

"We would have heard it take off," Pam reasoned.

"It may have taken off at the other end of the lake," said Uncle Russ.

"Or perhaps it broke away and is drifting on the water somewhere," Mr. Hollister suggested.

"But there wasn't any wind last night," said the pilot. "I believe," he added, "that someone untied my plane."

Mr. Hollister spoke up. "This is a matter for the police."

"Please let me tell them," Pete begged.

When his father said yes, the boy ran all the way to the police station. The desk sergeant looked at him questioningly.

"We've lost a plane," Pete said, "and we'd like you to help us find it."

The sergeant thought Pete was joking. "You mean a toy plane?"

"No, a real one with pontoons," Pete replied, and told the sergeant what had happened.

"That's mighty serious," came the sober reply. The officer said he would radio to the Shoreham police cruiser on Pine Lake.

"Officer Cal is in charge of it today," the sergeant said.

When Pete reported this to the others, Holly cried, "Maybe we can all go with Officer Cal and help find the plane!"

Presently a speck appeared far out on the lake. As it grew larger, the Hollisters could see that it was the Shoreham police launch.

"Here comes Officer Cal!" Ricky shouted, dancing up and down on the dock. "Oh, I hope we can go."

The young officer steered directly to the dock, turned off the motor, and greeted the group. He was introduced to the Hollisters' visitors, then said, "Tell me just what happened."

After the policeman had heard the story, he said, "There's been other trouble like this recently. Several boats have been untied and allowed to drift on the lake. Perhaps the same prankster was fooling with your plane."

"Please may we go with you to look for it?" Ricky begged.

"Okay, jump in," Officer Cal invited.

Instantly Ricky, Holly, Pete, and Pam hopped into the launch.

"I have room for you men, too," Officer Cal said, so the two Hollisters and Pilot Jordan went aboard.

As they set off, Gram, Gramp, and Mrs. Hollister, who was holding Sue in her arms, waved to them from the dock.

"Bring back the plane," Sue cried, "so you can fly to Crestwood for the merry-go-rounds."

"That's right," said Pam. "If we don't find it, we can't go on the trip."

As the boat headed out into the lake, Pete said, "Where will you look first, Officer Cal?"

The policeman replied that a north wind had been

"We've lost a plane," Pete said.

blowing during the night. Therefore, he thought they should cruise around the south shore of the lake. There were so many coves that a plane could easily drift into one of them and not be noticed.

The boat's engine purred as the craft made its way along the shore, a few hundred feet from the beach. From time to time they passed other boats and whenever they did Pete would call out, asking if anyone had seen a runaway pontoon plane. But nobody had.

"You'd think somebody would have spotted it," Al Jordan said. "It's not easy to hide a plane."

"It might be easier than you think on this lake," Officer Cal said. "I'd better check my map. Pete, do you want to take over the wheel?"

The boy was delighted with the chance to drive the police launch. He changed seats and steered as Officer Cal opened a compartment and pulled out a folded map. He spread it out on his knees and traced the shore line of Pine Lake with his finger.

"Here's one place we haven't looked," the policeman said, pointing to an indentation. "It was named Buttonhook Cove long ago."

"If the plane drifted in there," Mr. Hollister said, "we certainly couldn't see it from the lake."

Officer Cal relieved Pete at the wheel and headed straight for the cove. Following the channel, Officer Cal steered to the left.

"Yikes, we've found it!" Ricky shouted, as they

spied the pontoon plane floating in a pocket of water.

"Thank goodness," said Al Jordan.

"That was a shrewd guess, Officer," Uncle Russ complimented him.

The policeman grinned and throttled back the motor, allowing the launch to drift slowly toward the plane. As they approached, Pete cried out, "Look! Somebody's inside!"

Just then the door flew open on the far side of the craft and a boy hopped down to the pontoons.

"Stop! Halt!" Officer Cal shouted.

But the boy, his face and most of his body concealed by the plane's wing, leaped onto the shore and disappeared into the woods.

"Did anybody get a good look at him?" the policeman asked.

No one had and Cal said, "It will be useless to chase him through the woods. Let's just hope he didn't damage the plane."

Al Jordan was the first one to climb aboard. After looking quickly about he called back to the others, "Everything seems to be all right. I guess that boy was just curious to see what the inside of a pontoon plane looks like."

"Do you want to fly back to the Hollisters' dock?" Officer Cal asked the pilot. "I can tow you out into open water."

The pilot said he thought not. It would be better to check the whole plane at the Hollisters'.

"*Everything seems to be all right.*"

"Then I'll tow you all the way," the policeman offered.

He opened a locker and pulled out a long coil of rope. With Pete and Ricky helping him, he looped it around the pontoon struts and tied it to the back of the police boat.

"Please may I ride in the plane and play pilot while you're towing it?" Ricky asked.

"And I'll be co-pilot," said Holly.

Al Jordan saw nothing wrong with this, so the brother and sister climbed into the cockpit. The motorboat started up and headed out of the cove, pulling the pontoon plane behind it.

"Wheee! This is fun!" Ricky shouted.

Holly sat beside him and kept a sharp lookout on

all sides for trouble. When they reached the Hollister dock, the plane was tied securely. Al Jordan thanked Officer Cal. Then he revved the plane's motor and declared it to be in perfect condition. After this he carefully examined the plane itself.

"Everything seems to be okay," he declared, "however, I'll take it up before we start."

"Goody!" Holly cried. "Now we can fly to Crestwood this afternoon."

After breakfast Gram suggested that while they were waiting she and the girls start work on the toys and dolls for the fair.

"We'll cut out rag dolls first," Gram decided.

"Are they going to have buttons for eyes and nose?" Sue asked, as the shears wound in and out of the material.

"You can make one that way," Gram said, and Sue giggled excitedly at the thought.

Holly and Pam decided they would paint faces on the dolls they made. After they had worked for an hour, Pam reminded her sisters that she had promised to help at the day nursery. She had an early lunch and set out. When she arrived, the first children she looked for were Jack and Jill Byrd. Pam found the twins hugging their mother, who was seated in a chair looking very sad.

"What's the matter, Mrs. Byrd?" Pam asked.

At first the woman did not answer, but then, realizing how kind and sympathetic Pam was, she said, "I lost my job today. The factory where I worked

"May the twins stay with me?" Pam said.

closed down. I don't know what I'll do to support the twins."

"Maybe my dad can help you find a job," Pam offered hopefully.

Mrs. Byrd said that the trouble was she was not very strong and was not supposed to do any hard work. Right now she was going to a distant point to see if relatives could help support the twins.

"While I'm gone Mrs. Griffith will keep Jack and Jill here," she said. "I hope to be back by Thursday evening, so Mrs. Griffith can attend her nephew's wedding."

"If you don't get back, perhaps Jack and Jill can stay at our house," Pam offered.

"Yes, please, Mommy," Jill said. "I like Pam."

"Me, too," said Jack.

Mrs. Byrd smiled in spite of her sadness and thanked Pam. Then, rising, she kissed the twins good-by.

Pam spent the next two hours helping with games and puzzles and playing with the children in the big back yard. Before she knew it, the time to start for home arrived, and she hurried off.

As she started up the walk of her home, Mr. Hollister, who had hurried off to *The Trading Post* as soon as the airplane had been discovered, pulled into the driveway. They went into the house together.

"All set for the flight to Crestwood?" he called out.

"Yes, we are," the rest of the family chorused.

Suitcases were carried from the house to the plane and stowed aboard. Mrs. Hollister had telephoned to Aunt Marge to let her know they were coming.

"Teddy and Jean are so excited," she said. "They can hardly wait to see you children again."

After good-bys had been said all around, and, as Sue put it, she had been kissed umpty-nine times, the passengers took their seats.

"Take good care of Gram and Gramp," Pam called to her little sister.

"I know they'll behave for me," Sue said, giggling, and waved to the others.

The door was closed. With a roar the engine started and the propeller whirled. Then Pilot Jordan taxied out onto the lake.

The pontoons skimmed over the water. This time, however, the pilot had to make a longer take-off because there were so many people in his plane. Finally he pulled back on the wheel and up they went!

It seemed to the children that Pine Lake was traveling away from them and that they were standing still.

"Good-by, Shoreham!" Holly said, waving, as the lake disappeared from sight.

The plane rose higher and higher over the beautiful wooded country below.

"That sure is a sweet motor," Pete said, listening to the rhythmical throb it made.

But no sooner had he said this when a high whining

66

sound was heard. The children looked at one another.

"What's that noise?" Ricky asked.

It stopped for a second, then was heard again.

"Do you suppose," Pam wondered, "that something's wrong with the plane's engine after all?"

CHAPTER 7

Trouble

WHAT could the strange whining sound in the plane be? If something were wrong with the engine, surely the pilot would know about it. But he did not seem to be worried.

"Sounds as if it might be coming from the baggage compartment," Pete said.

"Let's look," Ricky proposed.

The brothers opened the small door at the rear of the cabin. On top of the suitcases sat White Nose, the Hollisters' cat!

"Meow! Meow!" White Nose cried. She jumped out and landed in Holly's arms.

"White Nose is a stowaway!" she giggled.

The Hollisters decided that White Nose must have jumped aboard the plane unnoticed when the others were saying good-by. The cat continued to meow as the plane sped through the sky, and finally Ricky said, "I guess White Nose doesn't like riding in a plane."

The cat put her left paw to one ear and rubbed it. Then she did the same with the other.

"I think the vibration from the engine is bothering her," Pete suggested.

"But I can fix that," Holly declared.

The pigtailed girl took a handkerchief from her pocket and folded it into a triangle. She tied this around White Nose's head, covering the cat's ears. It looked like a tiny cocked hat.

"That will keep the noise out," Holly told her, stroking White Nose.

The cat shook her head several times, but, seeing that the little hat would not come off, seemed content to wear it.

"See, she's happier already," Holly said, as the cat snuggled down in her lap and closed her eyes.

Two hours later the plane began to circle over a snug little town.

"It's Crestwood!" Pam cried. "And there's our old school!"

The plane landed on the Crestwood River and, as Al Jordan taxied up to the big town dock, the Hollister children could see pretty, dark-haired Aunt Marge and their cousins waiting for them.

Teddy and Jean waved excitedly as the plane pulled up beside them. Jean was nine years old and a pal of Pam's. She had straight chestnut-colored hair and dimples. Jean loved animals and had a pair of cocker spaniels and a pony.

Her brother, Teddy, eleven, had black hair and

"That will keep the noise out, White Nose."

gray eyes. He was just as lively as Pete and looked somewhat like him, although he was an inch shorter.

They greeted their relatives enthusiastically; then Aunt Marge said, "We're awfully happy to see you, but I'm afraid we have bad news."

"What happened?" Mrs. Hollister asked in concern.

"It's about Mr. De Marco," said Aunt Marge. "He telephoned several times today to speak to you."

"What does he want?" Pete said, worried.

His aunt hesitated before replying. Then she sighed and said, "Mr. De Marco doesn't think he can let you have his merry-go-round after all."

"What!" The Hollisters groaned.

"Why did he change his mind? What did he say?" Pete asked excitedly.

71

Aunt Marge said the man would not give any reason. "But he wants to see you right away."

The boys helped unload the baggage from the plane. Then they said good-by to Mr. Jordan and he took off.

The Hollisters walked to Uncle Russ's sedan and got in. It was a tight fit for ten people, so Ricky and the girls had to sit on the others' laps. It was not for long, however. In a few minutes they arrived at Uncle Russ's home, located on the outskirts of Crestwood.

It was a low rambling ranch-type house on several acres of land. Behind it was a barn where Teddy and Jean kept their pony and dogs.

"We'll go to Mr. De Marco's at once," said Uncle Russ. "But this time we'll take two cars and have plenty of room."

After the luggage had been taken out, they set off. Uncle Russ drove the sedan with the men and boys as passengers while his wife took Mrs. Hollister and the girls in her convertible.

Mr. De Marco lived in an old-fashioned house. Behind it was a two-story barn with a weather vane. The visitors pulled into the driveway and mounted the porch steps. Then Pete banged the knocker.

The door was opened by a short, stout, gray-haired man in a dressing gown and slippers. His face was rather pale and to the children he seemed very stern as he said, "You are the Hollisters, I presume."

"Yes, we are," Pete's father replied, smiling, and introduced both families. "We have come all the way from Shoreham for the merry-go-rounds. But I understand you may not let us take them."

"That's right," the owner said. He looked at each one of the Hollisters from Shoreham, then added, "I don't like to be fooled."

"What do you mean?" Pete cried. "We haven't fooled anyone."

"Come inside and I'll tell you," the man said, slowly leading the way into a large, comfortable living room.

A small, gray-haired woman, wearing a flowered apron, entered and Mr. De Marco introduced her as his wife.

"Please sit down, all of you," she said, "and Poppa will tell you why he is displeased."

The Hollisters listened quietly while he told them

The children told him about the school fair.

73

about two men who had called on him the day before. They had offered to buy his large merry-go-round.

"I told them it was not for sale," Mr. De Marco said, "and besides, I was lending it to you. The men told me you planned to make money for yourselves with it."

"Oh, that's not true!" Pam exclaimed. "Really, Mr. De Marco, it is for our school fair and all the money we make is going to a day nursery."

"How can I be sure of that?" the man asked.

"You can check with our school principal," Pete spoke up.

Mr. De Marco looked a bit uncomfortable. "Maybe that won't be necessary," he said.

The four children told him about plans for the school fair.

"It sounds nifty," said Teddy.

Finally a smile spread over Mrs. De Marco's face. Her husband, too, grinned. "I guess there's no doubt but that this is for charity. Forgive me for listening to those fellows."

"By the way, what were their names?" Mr. Hollister asked.

When Mr. De Marco said he did not know, Uncle Russ suggested he describe them. As he began, the cartoonist pulled out a pad and pencil and started to sketch. The carrousel owner described one man as of medium height with a thin face, short nose, and heavy, bushy eyebrows.

The second man, he said, was taller, with a long

"We'll spy on the Hollisters," one man said.

nose, hollow cheeks, and a goatee. When Mr. De Marco finished, Uncle Russ held the sketches toward him.

"Do these look anything like those fellows?"

The gray-haired man gave a startled gasp. He turned to his wife. "Mamma," he said, "see here. These look just like the two who wanted to buy my big merry-go-round."

Mrs. De Marco nodded. "You would make a good detective, Mr. Russ Hollister," she said.

"I'm not half as good at detective work as my brother John's children." The cartoonist laughed and turned toward them. "You should find these two scallawags who nearly ruined your plans."

"Yes," said Holly, "let's find Mr. Goatee and his friend."

"I wonder why they told such a big fib about us," Pete mused.

Mr. De Marco said that it might have been because they wanted the big merry-go-round themselves. Anyway, he would be happy to lend both merry-go-rounds for the fair. The Hollisters said they would come for them Monday morning.

Mr. De Marco took his visitors out to the barn to show them the merry-go-rounds. The large one was knocked down, so there was no chance to ride on it, but the children admired the various wooden animals that were piled up.

"Someday I'm going to ride that lion," Ricky declared, trying to get astride it.

The next moment he and the whole pile tumbled to the floor!

"Look out, Rick! They're alive!" Pete teased.

The younger children took turns riding on the small attractive merry-go-round set upon the trailer.

"Oh, isn't it wonderful?" Pam cried. "We're lucky, Mr. De Marco."

The man smiled and his wife said, "Before you go, I have a treat for you."

She went for a plate of cakes in the shape of twisted crullers, covered with honey and colored sprinkles.

"Oh, yum," Ricky said, biting into his.

"Mamma makes these every year around Easter time," Mr. De Marco said proudly. "I only wish my doctor would let me eat more of them!"

After they had eaten the cakes, the children and their parents left the De Marco home. The cousins played together the rest of the evening and the next day went to church. After dinner, Pam said, "Mother, may we visit our old home?"

"I think that would be very nice," Mrs. Hollister said.

The six children walked to the house. Several of their old friends greeted them on the way and went along.

"Let's play hide-and-seek," Pam suggested when they reached the house. She wanted to do this because she remembered a secret hiding place in a thick hedge at the back of the property.

Ricky volunteered to be *it*. Hiding his eyes with

his arms he counted up to one hundred and the children scooted in all directions. Pam ran directly to the hedge.

"Here I come, ready or not!" Ricky cried.

Suddenly Pam heard voices on the other side of the hedge. Two men were standing on the sidewalk a little distance away, with their backs turned.

"We mustn't let those Hollisters out of our sight," one said. "We'll spy on them."

Pam was startled. Who were they? Try as she might, the girl could not get a good look at the men's faces, so she stepped from her hiding place.

Evidently the men heard her, because they ran to a green car, jumped in, and sped away down the street.

Worried, Pam ran back to tell the others.

CHAPTER 8

A Merry-Go-Round Chase

EXCITEDLY Pam told her cousins and playmates about the two strange men who had said they must keep an eye on the Hollisters.

"I wish you'd seen them," said Pete. "And Dad should know about this. Maybe they're spying on him, too."

The children said good-by to their playmates and ran all the way to Uncle Russ's house. The grownups were in the back yard. Pam quickly told them what had happened.

"This is amazing," Mr. Hollister said.

"Dad, do you think these might be the same men who told the false story to Mr. De Marco?" Pete asked.

"It might be. It certainly is a big mystery."

Aunt Marge sighed. "I hope you don't have any trouble with those men on your way back to Shoreham. Please promise me that you'll always be on the lookout for them."

"We will, dear," Mrs. Hollister assured her, and they all went inside for supper.

Uncle Russ asked the police to watch the house for any strange characters around, but no one was spotted during the night.

"I think Ricky and I should ride with Mother for protection," Pete said, at breakfast, "just in case those two fellows try to bother us."

This was agreed upon, and the girls would ride in the truck with Mr. Hollister. Uncle Russ, Aunt Marge, Teddy, and Jean drove their relatives to Mr.

"Good-by and good luck!"

De Marco's home. The carrousel man greeted them warmly and walked back to the barn with them. Unlocking the big doors, he rolled them open.

"Everything's ready to go," he said.

In the big truck were the animals and the various parts of the large merry-go-round which had to be put together. Pete was amazed by the gears and all the machinery to be assembled.

"Crickets, Dad," he said, "do you think we can get that together in Shoreham?"

Mr. De Marco overheard the question and smiled. "Here is a chart which will show you how to do it."

Mr. Hollister climbed into the big truck and drove it out of the barn. Then, with the boys helping, he and Uncle Russ pulled out the trailer with the small merry-go-round and attached it to the back of Uncle Russ's sedan.

"Well, I guess we're ready to leave," Mr. Hollister said. He shook hands with Mr. De Marco and promised to bring the machines back in good condition after the school fair was over.

Amid cries of good-by and good luck the Shoreham visitors drove off. Mrs. Hollister led the way with the small merry-go-round. Everybody was excited except White Nose. The cat jumped into the back seat of the sedan and stretched out for a nap.

As the strange-looking cavalcade of merry-go-rounds drove out of Crestwood, passers-by waved to the Hollisters. Soon they were in open country, riding up and down over low rolling hills. In order to pass the time, Pam and Holly decided to play a game to see who would be the first to see a yellow convertible driven by a red-haired woman.

"Here comes a yellow convertible now!" Pam said gleefully.

A woman was driving it, but the car sped by so quickly that the children could not see what she looked like, so they turned around to look out the rear window.

"She was a brunette," Pam said, disappointed.

Suddenly the girls' attention was taken by a green car, traveling some distance behind them.

"It looks like the same one those two men raced off in yesterday," Pam said excitedly. "Maybe it's following us on purpose."

Mr. Hollister glanced into his rearview mirror. The car was too far behind for him to make out any of the details.

"I'll slow down and give him a chance to pass," he said. "If he doesn't do it, then we'll know he's interested in us."

The girls' father slowed down. So did the other driver, keeping the same distance between them. Mr. Hollister speeded up a bit. The green car did the same.

"He's watching us, all right."

Pam asked, "How can we get a look at those two men? I have Uncle Russ's sketches with me." She pulled them out of her pocket.

"If one of them is Mr. Goatee, we'll know," Holly declared.

"I think there's a way of seeing them," Mr. Hollister said.

Honking his horn, he signaled to his wife, who was not far ahead, to stop. As the merry-go-round truck and the car pulled off to the side of the road, Mr. Hollister hopped out and ran forward. He told the others about the green car.

"Yikes! This is just like a police case," Ricky said.

Mr. Hollister suggested that as soon as their truck and car passed over the brow of the next hill, they should turn into the first side road.

"If we do it quickly enough," he said, "the men may not see us and drive right past. Maybe we can get a look at them then."

Meanwhile the green car had stopped some distance back. When the merry-go-round cavalcade started up again, so did the other driver. Half a mile ahead was a steep hill. After Mrs. Hollister reached the far side, Pete exclaimed, "What luck!"

Not far ahead was a dirt road which led off to the left through a patch of woods.

"Turn in, Mother, quick!" Ricky cried.

Mrs. Hollister signaled to her husband with her hand and turned into the lane which had a sharp curve in it. The truck followed immediately and was concealed from the road.

Pam and Pete jumped out and raced back toward

the main road. Then they hid behind a big rock and waited. A few seconds later *whizzz!* The green car sped past.

The driver was wearing a goatee!

Immediately Pam and Pete dashed back to their parents.

"It was Mr. Goatee!" Pam announced.

Mr. Hollister frowned. "If so, I hope they're off our trail now."

"It feels awful creepy to be followed," Holly remarked.

"Well, let's get back on the road again," her father said.

Mrs. Hollister drove along the lane until she found a clearing in which to turn around. Then she started slowly for the highway. Mr. Hollister, in order to give her room to pass, had to pull far to the side of the dirt road.

"Look out for the ditch, Dad!" Holly shouted.

Her warning came too late! The right wheels of the truck slid into the ditch!

"Oh-oh, he's stuck!" Ricky cried, jumping out of the car.

He was right, and finally Mr. Hollister said, "We'll have to find someone to pull us out. Did any of you notice if we passed a garage?"

They could not recall any, but Pete said, "I saw someone plowing a field with a tractor on the other side of the hill. Maybe he could help us."

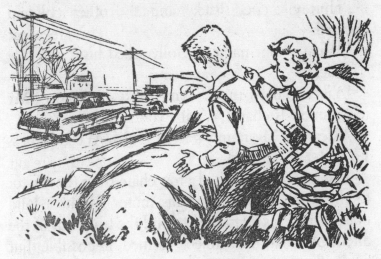

"It was Mr. Goatee."

Mr. Hollister said he would walk back and find out. Reaching the field, he saw a husky boy not much older than Pete driving the tractor. His blue jeans were faded and he wore a wide-brimmed straw hat.

"Hello, there," Mr. Hollister called.

The boy stopped the motor and looked over.

"We're in a little trouble," Mr. Hollister said, and explained the situation. "Can you pull the truck out?"

"Sure, mister, I'll be glad to." The boy smiled broadly.

Unhitching the plow from the tractor, he turned the vehicle around and drove toward the road. Mr. Hollister hopped onto the toolbox and it did not take them long to reach the truck.

"Hurray!" cried Ricky and the other children cheered.

"What's your name?" Holly asked him.

"Ricky."

"Yikes! That's mine," said Ricky Hollister. "My real name's Richard. What's yours?"

"Ricardo. My family's from Cuba. Well, I guess I'd better get to work."

The farm boy attached a tow chain from the tractor to the truck, then started his motor. What a loud noise it made as it strained to pull the truck out of the ditch! At first the project seemed impossible but finally there was a little movement of the wheels.

"There she goes!" Ricky yelled, as the truck moved ahead a few inches.

The tractor worked hard and all the Hollisters shoved. Several minutes later the truck was back on the road again. The farm boy hopped off the tractor and detached the chain.

"There you go," he said.

Mr. Hollister reached into a pocket and pulled out some money for Ricardo.

"No, thanks," said the lad. "I'm only too glad to be of service to you." He stood for a moment admiring the merry-go-rounds. "Gee," he said, "it must be a lot of fun to own two merry-go-rounds."

The children explained that these were only borrowed for their school fair.

"That should be keen!" the farm boy said, and added, "The last ride I had on a merry-go-round was

The Hollisters shoved.

at the Jumbo Carnival. It was here last spring, but I haven't seen it this year yet."

He jumped back on his tractor and drove off. As he did a strange look came over Pam's face.

"Jumbo Carnival?" she said aloud. "Do you suppose those men in the green car are from the Jumbo Carnival?"

"They could be," Pete added. "Perhaps those fellows are trying to get the merry-go-round for the carnival!"

"And cause us more trouble," Pam said, worried.

CHAPTER 9

A Night Visitor

ROLLING along again on the highway, the Hollisters could see no sign of the two men in the green car. Several hours later they stopped for a snack at a roadside restaurant. When they finished eating and were about to set off again, Pete said, "Let's change places now," and added with a smile, "Mr. Goatee and his friend have gone, so Mother won't need me and Ricky to protect her."

"Yes, let's," said Pam.

Holly climbed into the back seat of the sedan with White Nose, while her sister got in front with Mrs. Hollister. Pete and Ricky rode with their father, keeping a sharp lookout for the green car.

Late in the afternoon Mrs. Hollister signaled to her husband that she was going to stop at a big, white dairy bar. She pulled up in front of it and the truck also stopped.

"We'll rest here and have ice-cream cones," Mrs. Hollister told her family after she slid out from behind the steering wheel.

"Yippee!" Ricky shouted.

He ran on ahead and opened the big glass door of the air-conditioned building. Mrs. Hollister and the girls entered first with the others following. They seated themselves on a row of stools in front of a low, gleaming counter.

Ricky was so happy that he spun around three times on his stool. Whoops! Off it came and he fell to the floor!

He rewound it and sat down a little shamefaced as a pretty young woman in a white uniform asked them what they would like to have.

"A white ice-cream cone," Holly piped up.

"I'll have a black one," Ricky said.

"Make mine pink," Mrs. Hollister added.

"I'll have a purple one," Pam said.

"Yellow for me," was Pete's request.

Mr. Hollister grinned. "I'll take orange."

In a minute the waitress had the cones ready. They were vanilla, chocolate, strawberry, raspberry, lemon, and orange.

Suddenly Holly remembered White Nose and said, "May I please have a cone for our cat?"

"Of course," the girl replied, laughing.

Holly took it outside and held it for her pet, who lapped it so fast she got white drops on her whiskers.

When Holly returned, the waitress said, "Did you folks find the men in the green car who were looking for you?"

The chills that went up the Hollisters' spines were even colder than the ice cream.

"Looking for *us*?" Mr. Hollister exclaimed. "You're sure?"

Whoops! Off it came!

"Yes," the waitress replied. "Two men stopped here several hours ago and asked whether we had seen two merry-go-rounds pass along the road."

Pam showed the waitress the sketches Uncle Russ had made. "Yes, those are the men," the young woman said. "They seemed very eager to see you."

Mr. Hollister paid the bill and they started off. Again the two boys rode with their mother.

As it grew dark Mrs. Hollister said to them, "Doesn't this countryside look familiar to you?"

"Oh yes," Pete replied. "We stayed overnight near here when we moved to Shoreham."

"That's right," Ricky exclaimed, "and I think I see the motel up ahead there."

As they came closer to the place, Mrs. Hollister slowed down. "You're right. It's the same place.

Suppose we stay here overnight again. The owner was very nice to us."

The Hollisters drove into the courtyard, around which were located several cheery little cottages.

The motel owner was happy to see them again. "Well, well, the Happy Hollisters," he said, shaking Mr. Hollister's hand. Then he glanced about. "But where's the littlest girl?" he asked.

Pam told him that Sue was staying with her grandparents and the man said, "Next time bring her along, too. She tickles me."

He gave the visitors the same quarters they had had the last time. After unpacking their night clothes, the Hollisters ate a light supper at a new tearoom which the motel man had built several months before. When they finished, Mrs. Hollister suggested phoning to the folks in Shoreham.

"Please may I make the call?" Pam asked.

"All right," her mother said.

All of the Hollisters stood around the booth while Pam called long distance. Gram answered the phone and said that everything was fine at home. Then Sue got on the wire.

"Pam," she wailed, "I think someone has taken our cat. Please hurry home and help us look for White Nose."

"Oh dear," said Pam, "we should have let you know White Nose was a stowaway on the plane. She's fine, honey. You'll have her again tomorrow."

The little girl sighed in relief. Then she spoke to everyone in the family, telling her mother that she and Gram had made three tiny pies and a dozen elf cookies.

"We're saving them for you, Mommy," Sue told her.

After saying good-by to her, the Hollisters returned to the cabin. It was now dark, so they turned on the lights in the pretty cottage.

Suddenly there was a knock on the door. Mr. Hollister opened it. A man who stood there made every one of the Hollisters jump. He looked very much like one of the persons Uncle Russ had sketched!

Holly squeezed her mother's hand in fright as Mr. Hollister asked, "Yes, what can I do for you?"

"I want to buy your large merry-go-round," the man said.

"I'm sorry, but it's not for sale," the children's father replied.

"I'll give you plenty for it," the stranger persisted.

When Mr. Hollister explained that he did not own the merry-go-round, the man's face clouded up. He was about to make a reply when Holly said, "You're one of the men who visited Mr. De Marco, aren't you?"

The caller's eyes nearly popped out when he heard this. His jaw dropped and he shuffled uncomfortably.

"Where's your friend, Mr. Goatee?" Ricky asked.

This was too much for the man. Without another word he turned on his heel and ran off into the darkness.

"He certainly acted guilty," Mr. Hollister said, peering outside.

"Let's catch him and find out what's behind all this!" Pete proposed.

Mr. Hollister agreed. "Come on, boys!"

But by the time they ran to their sedan for a flashlight, the strange man had disappeared. The Hollisters looked all over the motel grounds but could find no trace of him. They returned to the cabin.

"I think you frightened him away," Mrs. Hollister said. Nevertheless, everyone was a little nervous about the caller.

Pete in particular found it hard to get to sleep because he kept listening for footsteps outside. Finally, however, he dozed off. But in the middle of the night he jumped up with a start. The boy heard the starter of a truck going rrrr-rrrr-rrrr.

"Dad! Mother!" Pete shouted, pounding on their door. "Someone's trying to take our truck!"

Mr. Hollister jumped out of bed and switched on the light. Then, sliding into bathrobe and slippers, he and Pete dashed out the door to the parking place where they had left the merry-go-rounds.

The hood of their truck was up and a man was bending over the motor. Was he the stranger who had called on them?

Pete and his father sprinted after the man.

When he heard the Hollisters coming, the man dashed off without their seeing his face. Pete and his father sprinted after him. But a car, its motor running, was waiting at the roadside. The man hopped in and it sped off.

"We mustn't let him get away!" Mr. Hollister said with determination. "We'll chase the fellow in our sedan."

Quickly he and the boys unhitched the small merry-go-round from it. By this time all the Hollisters and several other people in the motel had been aroused and come to find out what had happened.

"Somebody tried to steal our merry-go-round truck!" Pete told them. "We're going after him!"

Ricky begged to go, so his father said, "Hop in. But the rest of you had better stay here and guard the truck."

Mr. Hollister drove onto the main highway and roared along in search of the getaway car. They picked up a taillight and began to close the distance between them.

"Fifty mile speed limit," Mr. Hollister read, and followed it closely.

As they neared the car ahead, Pete saw that it was not green, but black. Passing it, Mr. Hollister continued the chase. Half a mile farther on they could see another car in front of them.

"I think that's the one!" Pete said. "Come on, Dad! Let's catch them!"

But the other car seemed to be going nearly as fast as the Hollisters were. As they raced along, spatters of rain hit the windshield. Soon it was raining hard. Mr. Hollister turned on the wipers, which made a hissing sound as they cleared the drops from the glass.

"We're gaining on them, Dad," Pete called out.

"If that car doesn't slow down for that curve ahead, it may have trouble," his father said, slowing down himself.

The automobile ahead did not slow down. Suddenly it skidded on the slippery pavement. The tires screeched. The car swayed back and forth, then ran over an embankment!

The car ran over an embankment.

CHAPTER 10

A Low Tunnel

PETE cried out in alarm when the car in front of them skidded off the road. They watched it jounce into an open field and come to a stop.

"I hope nobody's hurt," Mr. Hollister said, pulling off the side of the road. He and the boys hurried across the field holding a flashlight.

Approaching the car, they saw that the doors were opening. Much to their surprise, a man and a woman got out.

"Are you hurt?" Mr. Hollister asked.

"Crickets!" Pete whispered. "These aren't the people we were looking for."

"Are you hurt?" Mr. Hollister asked, running up to them.

"My wife bumped her head, but I don't think it's serious," the man replied.

"We thought you were someone else," Pete confessed. "We were trailing two men in a green car which looks something like yours."

Mr. Hollister offered to help the man get his car back on the road. "You steer the wheel," he suggested, "and my sons and I will push you over the rough spots."

The man got into the car. It was difficult to drive over the field and several times the rear wheels mired into the soft earth. But Pete, Ricky, and their father put their shoulders to the rear of the car and pushed it until they reached the road.

"Thanks so much for helping us," the woman said, as she got in and they drove off.

"I think Mr. Goatee and his friend have outdistanced us by now," Pete said ruefully.

His father agreed that further chase would be useless, so they drove back to the motel and reported their failure.

The next morning before the Hollisters started out, Pam consulted the road map. "Dad," she said, pointing, this road looks as if it might be a short cut to Shoreham."

"We'll take it," Mr. Hollister said. "Besides

getting home sooner, it'll keep us away from Mr. Goatee and his friend."

After a breakfast of cereal, bacon and eggs, Mr. Hollister and the boys hitched the small merry-go-round onto the back of the sedan, and the carrousel caravan drove off. They followed the road Pam had suggested. It wound through the beautiful countryside along an old canal. Presently they came to a high embankment.

"Look, Mother," said Ricky, who was riding with her and Pete, "the canal goes right over the road." Before them was a low, narrow tunnel.

"Goodness, I wonder if Dad can get the truck through here," Mrs. Hollister said, slowing down as she passed through the tunnel, and looked in her rearview mirror.

Mr. Hollister proceeded to drive the truck slowly through the tunnel, but suddenly there was a scraping sound.

"The merry-go-round is hitting the top of the tunnel!" Holly cried, leaning out of the truck window and looking up.

"You'll never get through!" Pam warned her father.

"Let's give it one more try," Mr. Hollister said. The truck inched forward but the scratching sound continued. "No go!" he finally admitted. "I'll have to back out of this tunnel."

Putting the truck into reverse he started backward, but when they had gone only a few feet there was another crunching noise and the truck stopped.

"Oh, we're stuck!" Pam wailed.

Meanwhile two other cars had pulled up in back of the carrousel truck and began to honk their horns impatiently.

"This is a fine kettle of fish!" Mr. Hollister said with a wry grin. "I can't go forward and I can't go backward either."

"Maybe I can help you, Daddy," Holly said. "If I climb on top of the load maybe I can jiggle some of the merry-go-round parts lower so we can back out."

Pam offered to help, too, but because Holly was smaller, her father agreed to let her try. She stepped out of the truck's cab and went up the side of the vehicle like a monkey.

When she reached the top Holly called down, "Oh, I see what's the matter. The nose of one of the horses is rubbing against the top of the tunnel."

Holly rocked the wooden animal back and forth. "Okay, Daddy, try it again," she said.

Mr. Hollister backed up again. This time the load cleared the top of the tunnel by a fraction of an inch. He backed out safely and allowed the other cars to pass through.

Pam felt sorry about the short cut she had chosen. Now they would lose a lot of time.

"That's all right, dear," her father said. "We'll find another way."

Meanwhile Mrs. Hollister had turned around and

come back through the tunnel. Both vehicles stopped along the road and they quickly scanned the map for another route.

"Here's one," Mrs. Hollister said, pointing to a winding road. She added, "Oh dear, instead of gaining time I'm afraid now it will take us longer than ever to reach Shoreham."

The country road proved to be full of little dips which Mrs. Hollister told the boys were called "Thank you, ma'ams."

"It's like a roller coaster!" said Pete.

When it drew near lunch time, Mrs. Hollister pulled into a tiny roadside refreshment stand. In front of it were a few tables shaded by a towering oak tree.

"This'll be a yummy place to eat," Holly said, as a young woman approached them with a menu in her hands.

"We don't have much of a choice," the waitress said, smiling, "but I would recommend you try our delicious hamburgers."

"Good!" the children cried and everybody ordered hamburgers and milk.

While they were eating, two tots walked shyly up to the table. The woman ordered them away, saying they were her little nephew and niece.

"Oh, let them stay here and talk to our children," Mrs. Hollister said.

The boy, who was three years old, was named Roy.

"Thanks for the ride," little Roy said.

His sister Thelma was four. After they had talked to the children awhile, Thelma said, "Would you give us a ride on your merry-go-round?"

"I want to yide the yiddle one," Roy said, pointing a chubby finger at the carrousel on the trailer.

"I don't know that we'll have enough time," Mrs. Hollister said.

This made little Roy burst into tears. His sister joined him. What a noise there was!

"Oh dear," said Pam, "these poor little things want a ride so badly. Don't you suppose we could do it for them?"

"Please, Daddy," said Holly, "let's start the little merry-go-round."

"All right," Mr. Hollister said. "Roy and Thelma may have a ride."

Almost instantly the two children stopped crying. They smiled, though tears still glistened in their eyes.

Mr. Hollister started a gasoline motor which turned the small merry-go-round. The two children got on, Thelma selecting a toy deer and Roy a horse. The merry-go-round was a six-seater, so the four Hollisters hopped on, too.

Around and around they went, shouting joyfully. After a good, long ride, Mr. Hollister stopped the carrousel and the children got off.

"Thanks for the yide," Roy said.

"He means ride," his sister told the Hollisters.

"That's what I said—yide!" Roy repeated.

Mr. Hollister paid the woman for the lunch, explaining that they were eager to get home.

"Maybe I can help you," the woman said. "There's a new road not far from here which has just been completed. It connects with the main highway to Shoreham."

"That is a help," Mr. Hollister said as she showed him the directions on the map.

Mrs. Hollister found the new road without any trouble and both the car and the truck breezed along the way to Shoreham, making good time. The sun was low in the west when they passed a sign reading, *Welcome to Shoreham.*

"Hurray, hurray, we're home!" Ricky shouted. It was not long before they pulled into the Hollister driveway.

Sue dashed out to meet them and jumped into

her mother's arms. "Merry-go-rounds!" she squealed.

Gram and Gramp hurried outside too. "Goodness, you have a regular circus here," Gramp said. "They look very fine."

It was not long before other neighborhood children raced into the Hollisters' yard. They all begged for a ride on the small merry-go-round and Mr. Hollister set it going again.

Pete and Pam, meanwhile, had just come outside after carrying some luggage into the house, when Officer Cal drove up in his police car. He got out and crossed the lawn where Mr. Hollister was standing.

The policeman looked very embarrassed as he said, "Mr. Hollister, we just received a telephone call at headquarters from a man named Byrd. He says you're operating a merry-go-round without a license and thinks you should be arrested!"

CHAPTER 11

A Cruel File

THE Hollisters could hardly believe what Officer Cal had said. "Who wants me to be arrested?" the children's father asked.

"A man named Zack Byrd," the policeman said as Sue ran up and leaped into his arms. "He's half owner of the Jumbo Carnival, I understand."

Sue hugged the officer. "You don't arrest anybody but bad people, do you?" she asked.

"That's right," Cal replied, grinning. "This fellow Byrd is mistaken about the whole thing, but just to clear matters, why don't we all go down to headquarters?"

The Hollisters got into their car and drove with their father to the police station. He told his story to the captain and added that somebody had been trying to get the large carrousel away from them. Then he asked if it would be necessary for Pete and the other boys who were going to run the merry-go-round for the school fair to have a license.

"No," the captain replied.

"Mr. Byrd is an old meany," Holly declared. "Maybe he's one of the men who tried to buy the merry-go-round from Mr. De Marco."

"And he might be the same one who came to the motel," Pam said.

"And then we think he tried to steal it," Pete added.

"This is serious," the captain said. "I'll summon Mr. Byrd and have a talk with him. He's at the Empire Hotel."

The captain phoned the hotel and in ten minutes Mr. Byrd arrived.

At once Holly burst out with, "See I told you he's one of the men Uncle Russ made a sketch of!"

Mr. Byrd looked very stern as he faced the police captain and was told that his charge against the Hollisters was unfounded.

"And furthermore," the officer said, "it's suspected

"The Hollisters are trying to ruin my business!"

you tried to steal the big merry-go-round which the Hollisters brought from Crestwood."

"I didn't!" Mr. Byrd cried out, glaring at the Hollisters. "I only tried to buy it."

"Then was it your friend with the goatee who did try to get away with the truck Monday night?" Pete demanded.

"We had nothing to do with it," Mr. Byrd declared. "The Hollisters are just trying to ruin my business, that's what they're doing!"

The police chief said he hoped they would get the mystery untangled soon. With that, Mr. Byrd stalked out of the police station.

"I think I'd better keep an eye on him just the same," Officer Cal said. "At least until the school fair is over."

Mr. Hollister asked the chief where he thought the large carrousel might be parked, saying there was room in the Hollisters' yard for only the small one. The captain suggested that the big merry-go-round be taken to the Board of Education garage which was adjacent to Lincoln School. Just before bedtime the boys and their father drove it there.

"I can hardly wait to set it up," said Pete.

"I'll be the first rider." Ricky grinned.

The next morning all the Hollister children except Sue were so weary that they overslept.

"Hurry!" Mrs. Hollister called upstairs to them, "or you'll be late for school."

They dressed quickly and after a hasty breakfast

scooted out the front door. They arrived at Lincoln School just as the bell was ringing.

When their teachers asked Pete and the others why they had been absent, the Hollisters proudly told about their trip to Crestwood and the merry-go-rounds they had brought back. They were praised for this, then told to bring written excuses from home the next morning.

About eleven o'clock, each of them was summoned to the principal's office. They met on the way.

"Crickets, I wonder what's going on?" Pete said.

"Maybe Mr. Russell wants to thank us for getting the merry-go-rounds," Pam suggested cheerfully.

The four children stepped inside the principal's office and a secretary ushered them into Mr. Russell's private room.

"Sit down," he said, then added, "I sent for you to find out why you children played hooky Monday and Tuesday."

The Hollisters looked thunderstruck. "We weren't playing hooky!" Pete spoke up.

"That's the report I received," Mr. Russell said, frowning.

"We weren't even in town," Pam said. "We were riding back from Crestwood with two merry-go-rounds."

Ricky told the whole story in a straightforward manner.

"That's strange," Mr. Russell replied. "Joey Brill reported to me that you were playing around your

They arrived as the bell was ringing.

home all day yesterday. And," he added, tapping a pencil on his desk, "I didn't receive any excuses from your parents."

Holly explained that they had not had time to bring notes from home and added, "If you call up Daddy you'll find out we're telling the truth."

"That won't be necessary," Mr. Russell said. "I'll see Joey after school instead."

"It was a mean trick," Holly declared.

"I'll grant it was," Mr. Russell replied. Then he added, "Thank you very much for getting the merry-go-rounds. I'm sure they'll be a big addition to our school fair."

On the way home for lunch that noon, Ricky noticed that Joey Brill was walking close behind him. Catching up, the bully said, "I know somebody who's going to stay after school today for playing hooky."

A twinkle came into Ricky's eyes. "You do?" he said, raising his eyebrows. "Well, I know somebody who's going to stay after school today for telling fibs."

Joey's jaw fell when he heard this. He said no more and hurried off. The other Hollisters laughed when they heard the joke.

After school Ricky ran home to work on his soapbox car. When he reached the garage he found Holly and Gramp there. Holly was grooming Domingo. Gramp was greasing the axles of the derby car.

"You've made a mighty fine start," Gramp told the boy. "But we'll need more parts."

"Like a steering wheel, you mean?" Ricky asked.

"That's right. And I know where we can get one," Gramp replied. He told Ricky that there was a junk yard on the outskirts of a nearby town.

"Let's drive over and take a look," Ricky said enthusiastically.

Gramp's eyes twinkled. "We might even pick up a fancy grille for your radiator."

Since the station wagon was not being used by anyone that afternoon, Gramp drove Ricky to the junk yard in it.

"Yikes!" his grandson exclaimed as they got out. "This is keen!"

The place was full of old automobiles. Some had the tops off, others were without wheels.

"This auto was built for a midget."

"Something I can do for you?" a man in overalls asked them, walking up.

"We'd like a steering wheel," Ricky said, "for my soap-box racer."

"And a nice shiny radiator grille, too," Gramp said, winking at the man.

"I think I have just the things for you," came the reply. "Follow me."

He led the Hollisters to the rear of the junk yard, past piles of rusty fenders and worn-out engines. Then they came to a little car which was partly dismantled.

"This auto was built for a midget," the junk man said. "He parked it on a hill one day, but the brake wasn't set tight. The car rolled down and hit a tree. Now look at it!"

The little auto was a sorry-looking sight. Apparently it had been almost brand new before the accident, because it was still shiny. But it now lay in a bent twisted heap.

"What did the poor midget do after his car broke up?" Ricky asked.

"He had another one built," the man replied. "He works for a circus as a clown and makes plenty of money." The junk-yard owner laughed. "I guess a midget pays a midget price."

"Boy, this is nifty!" Ricky said, looking over the wrecked car. "It has a steering wheel just the right size for my racer."

"Wait here and I'll take it out for you," the man said, and went off for some tools.

In a few minutes he returned with a set of wrenches and went to work. Soon he had the steering wheel off the car and handed it over.

"Isn't it a beauty, Gramp?" Ricky asked.

His grandfather said it was just the thing for the soap-box racer. "Now how about some nice shiny trimmings for the body of your car?"

"Help yourself to that scrap of chromework over there," the junk dealer said, pointing to a heap lying nearby.

Ricky and Gramp selected some long shiny strips and Ricky picked out a piece of grillework that did not have even one dent in it.

"I don't know how fast your buggy will go," Gramp said, "but it sure will be one of the best looking in the race."

"Say, I have just the thing this lad would like," the man said. He went over to a very old automobile which Gramp laughingly said was probably made in the year one. He reached inside and unscrewed something and quickly handed it to Ricky.

"Yikes, an old horn!" Ricky said.

"Yes, it works by hand," the man replied. "Just the thing if you're going to make a soap-box racer."

Ricky pressed down on the knob on top of the horn and it went ooga-ooga.

"This will scare anybody out of the way," Ricky

said proudly, as Gramp paid for the purchases.

Ricky put his treasures into the back of the station wagon and Gramp started for home. They passed a meadow on the right side of the road just as they were about to enter Shoreham.

Ricky glanced over the field and in the distance saw two boys playing with what looked like a small horse. As he watched, they slapped the animal to make it go faster. Ricky did not like the treatment and said so.

"Gramp, do you think that's a pony?" he asked.

Gramp Hollister slowed down and looked to where his grandson was pointing.

"It doesn't look like a pony to me, Ricky," he said. "I think it's a donkey."

The two drove on, talking about the wonderful soap-box racer they were going to build. When they pulled into the driveway they saw Holly running into the house crying.

"I wonder what happened to her?" Ricky said, getting out of the car and following his sister through the back door.

"Mother! Mother!" Holly wailed.

"What has happened?" Mrs. Hollister said, grabbing the little girl in her arms.

"Domingo is gone!" Holly sobbed. "Our little donkey is gone!"

CHAPTER 12

Tracking Hoofprints

"Oh, SOMEBODY stole our burro!" Holly wailed. "I just went to feed him and he's gone!"

Gramp, who had come into the kitchen, said that maybe Domingo had only wandered off a short distance.

"Oh no. I've looked all 'round for him," the little girl insisted.

"We'll find him," Ricky said. Then suddenly he exclaimed, "Gramp, do you think that donkey we saw in the field could be Domingo?"

"We'll drive back to the place right away and find out," Gramp said. "Come along, Holly."

The brother and sister hopped into the station wagon and hurried toward the meadow.

"Those two boys might have been Joey Brill and Will Wilson," Ricky declared, as they neared the big field, "getting square with us because we found out Joey's trick."

"I'll bet they're trying to ruin our plan for giving rides at the school fair!" Holly said.

When they came to the meadow, Gramp stopped the car. The burro was nowhere in sight.

"He was right over there." Ricky pointed. "What say we pick up his hoofprints, Gramp? It ought to be easy."

The elderly man locked the car and the three hurried across the field to the place where Ricky had last seen the burro.

"Look!" Holly said, gazing at the soft ground. "Here are some marks just like our little donkey's."

"Let's go!" Ricky yelled, and led the way across the field. The trail of hoofmarks crossed the meadow and came to the edge of a little woods. Pressing in among the trees and bushes, the boy kept track of the marks made by the animal.

"Yikes!" said Ricky suddenly, "the prints are much deeper here. What does that mean, Gramp?"

The children and Gramp waded across the stream.

"I guess those boys got onto the burro's back and made him carry them."

"And I see why, too," Holly said, looking ahead to a wide, shallow stream.

"We'll go across, too," said Ricky firmly.

The two children and Gramp took off their shoes and socks. Gramp and Ricky rolled up the legs of their pants and waded across the stream. Putting on their shoes again, they hurried on.

The hoofmarks were easily picked up. A few minutes later the three searchers came out of the woods into another field. At the edge of it stood an old abandoned farmhouse and barn.

"The trail leads to that old barn," Ricky said. "Perhaps the boys hid our burro in it."

Creeping up quietly to the barn door, Ricky flung it open. They all rushed into the dim interior.

There in a stall stood Domingo tied to a post!

"Oh, my poor dear donkey!" Holly said, rushing up and throwing her arms around the animal's neck. Domingo twitched his ears and pawed the ground.

"*Ee-aw! Ee-aw!*" he brayed happily.

Ricky, meanwhile, scooted around the barn, looking for the two boys who had brought Domingo there. But he did not find them.

"Maybe they were going to keep Domingo here until after the fair was over," Holly said.

She untied the animal and led him out of the barn. As they walked back to the car, Holly said, "How will we get him home?"

Her grandfather said they could tie the burro's guide rope to the back of the station wagon and drive home slowly.

"Please, may I ride him?" Holly asked.

Gramp smiled. "All right, but be careful. It's dangerous to ride bareback on the open road. Ricky, you hold Domingo's guide rope."

Gramp raised the rear window of the station wagon. Ricky climbed in and held the end of the rope. Holly hopped onto the burro's back and Gramp drove slowly back to town. People along the way chuckled at the sight.

The following day after school Pam and Holly were to work with Gram on rag dolls for the fair. Sue came to join in the fun. Just before they started to work, the director of the nursery phoned Pam. She reported that Mrs. Byrd was not back yet from her trip.

"I'd like to go to my nephew's wedding this evening," she said, "and I haven't been able to find anyone to come here and stay with the twins. You mentioned that your family might be able to keep them for me."

"I'll ask Mother," Pam offered, hurrying off. Mrs. Hollister said she would be delighted to have the twins visit them overnight and Pam hastened to tell this to Mrs. Griffith. "We'll come for them at five o'clock."

"Thank you very much, Pam."

The girl hung up and went to the sunroom where

Gram had already started work on the rag dolls. Holly and Sue had cut-out front and back pieces on their laps.

"We leave the head open," Gram said, "so we can put the cotton stuffing inside."

Sue had trouble managing the needle, thread, and thimble all at the same time. But she worked hard and finally she cried out, "Look, mine's all finished."

"Fine!" Gram replied. "Bring it here, and I'll show you how to stuff it."

As Sue picked up the rag doll, her own skirt came with it!

Pam laughed. "You've sewed the doll to your dress!" he said.

Sue looked very funny and Holly teased, "The very latest kind of rag doll which you carry around on your skirt."

"I didn't mean to do it!" Tears came to Sue Hollister's eyes.

"Of course you didn't," Gram said, and, taking some shears, she snipped the threads which held the doll to Sue's skirt.

When it neared five o'clock, Pam exclaimed, "I nearly forgot! I must go for Jack and Jill. Gram, will you go with me?"

"Yes, dear," was the reply. Pam and her grandmother hurried over to the nursery.

"It's so nice of you to take Jack and Jill," Mrs. Griffith said, after Pam had introduced Gram. "They're ready to leave." Then she whispered,

"Leave the head open for stuffing."

"I'm worried about their mother. I haven't received any word from her since she left town to call on relatives."

"Oh, I hope nothing has happened to her," Pam said. "Who are her relatives?"

"She's looking for her brother-in-law. His name is Byrd and he runs a carnival that travels around. Perhaps she can't find him."

"His name is Byrd and he runs a carnival?" Pam repeated, her eyes wide with excitement. Quickly she told about the Jumbo Carnival and the Mr. Byrd who had tried to buy the merry-go-round. "He's right here in Shoreham!"

"He may be the same one," Mrs. Griffith replied in amazement. "I'll tell Mrs. Byrd as soon as she returns."

By this time Jack and Jill had their coats on. They said good night to Mrs. Griffith. Jack took Gram's hand and Jill took Pam's. Before long they were walking across the Hollisters' yard and up the front porch steps. Mrs. Hollister opened the door. "Aren't they sweet!" she exclaimed, bending down to greet Jack and Jill Byrd and leading them inside.

The twins were very shy as they looked wonderingly about the large house. Then Jill said fretfully, "I want mama!"

"Mother is away on a trip," Pam said, "but she'll come home soon."

"Jill doesn't want Mother," Jack spoke up. "She wants mama."

Holly gave her a ride.

Suddenly the little girl broke out in tears. "I want mama," she repeated over and over.

"Goodness, how can we stop Jill from crying?" Mrs. Hollister worried as she tried to comfort the twin.

"I'll get her a cookie," Holly offered, and skipped to the kitchen. She returned with a handful of sugar cookies for Jack and Jill. The girl ceased her crying while she nibbled, but as soon as the cookies were eaten, she started to cry for "mama" again.

Pete thought a ride on the merry-go-round would stop her, so the twins were taken into the yard and given a spin on the small carrousel. This dried Jill's eyes for a while, but when the ride was over, she wailed again. "I want mama!"

"Why don't you go get mama?" Jack asked the startled group.

"We don't know where she is," Holly answered. Trying to quiet the unhappy Jill, Holly gave her a ride on her back. She bucked like a bronco while Jill held her pigtails.

Then Ricky stood on his head and at the same time made a funny face, which looked even sillier because he was upside down.

Jill smiled a little, but burst out again when Ricky stood up. "Gee, I can't stand on my head all night," Ricky said, disappointed.

"I want mama! I want mama!" Jill wailed as if her heart would break.

"I simply don't know what to do," Mrs. Hollister said, bouncing the little girl up and down in her arms.

Suddenly Pam said, "Mother, I think I've figured it out," and ran upstairs.

CHAPTER 13

Donkey-in-the-Box

TAKING the steps two at a time, Pam dashed upstairs to her bedroom. She went straight to a low bookcase, on which sat six dolls in a row. Selecting a pretty, dimpled one with soft skin, she hurried downstairs.

"Is this what you want, honey?" she asked Jill, putting the doll in her arms.

Jill bent the doll's body forward and out came the word "mama!" Instantly Jill stopped crying and hugged the cuddly toy. "I left my own mama at the nursery," she said, "and I miss her."

"Yikes!" cried Ricky, putting his hand to his head and falling backward off a hassock. "Is *that* all she wanted?"

He immediately went for a toy fire engine for Jack and they all had fun until bedtime.

Pam told Jill she might take the doll to bed with her. "Her name's Nancy Rae and Santa Claus brought her to me when I was four years old."

The next morning Pam took charge of helping Jill dress, while Ricky and Pete assisted Jack. All the Hollisters walked to the nursery with them, then went on to school. In the playground they met Ann Hunter.

"I've been put in charge of advance ticket sales," she said, "and I've been waiting to tell you a good plan I have for selling a lot of tickets."

"What is it?" Pete asked.

Ann explained that for each five tickets anyone sold the salesman would get a free ride on the small merry-go-round.

"That's a nifty idea," said Pete, and his brother and sisters nodded agreement.

When the plan was announced in assembly, all the pupils cheered. And after school what a helter-skelter there was as the children raced off to sell tickets!

In an hour a boy appeared in the Hollister yard with money for five tickets he had sold. Ann took it and he hopped onto the merry-go-round. It was not long before the Hollister lawn was crowded with children. Everyone wanted a ride at once so he could run off and sell more tickets.

"Please stay in line for your turn," called out Pete, in charge.

As Ann collected the money, Pam seated the eager

riders. Ricky brought out a small record player and put on peppy tunes.

"The advance sale is wonderful!" Ann said a little later, counting the money.

Everybody was happy until Joey Brill sneaked through the crowd near where Holly was standing. He frightened her as he said suddenly, "I hear your donkey ran off and you can't find him."

Holly whirled around to face the boy. "Oh, we found him all right," she said.

"You did? Where?"

"In an old deserted barn," Holly said.

"How did you find out——" Joey started to say, then stopped.

Holly became suspicious. "Did you take him there?" she asked.

"Don't accuse me!" Joey scowled.

"And Will Wilson helped you!" Holly said.

At this Joey gave her a hard shove. Holly teetered backward toward the spinning merry-go-round as Joey raced off. If her head hit the merry-go-round she might be badly hurt!

Just in time Jeff Hunter saw what had happened and caught Holly.

"Why did Joey do that?" Pete cried angrily.

"Because I guessed he took Domingo."

Pete wanted to go after the bully and settle the matter then and there, but he was too busy with his job.

"Let's play a trick on him," Ricky suggested.

"Like dumping him in the lake?" Pete asked.

"I have a better idea." Ricky's eyes lighted up. "Come here, Pete."

He led his brother to a place where the others could not hear him and whispered in his ear.

"That's fine!" Pete said. "When?"

"Right away," Ricky said. "Dave Mead can run the merry-go-round. I'll go get what we need from my room."

He hurried into the house and returned a few minutes later with a small, square box. It contained a toy which he had received the Christmas before.

"See, it still works!" Ricky said, showing it to Pete.

"This ought to scare Joey."

He opened the catch. *Presto!* The top of the box flew up and a donkey's head appeared.

"*Ee-aw! Ee-aw!*" it said.

"That ought to scare Joey," Pete said, "but the rest of it will be more fun."

The brothers hurried off in the direction of Joey Brill's house, Pete carrying a bucket with a rope on it. Coming into the rear of the property from a back street they could see that no one was in the yard.

"There's a place right under the tree," Ricky said, pointing.

"Okay, you go put it there while I fill this bucket."

Pete scouted around until he found a hose faucet on the side of the house and filled the bucket with water. As Ricky kept a lookout, Pete climbed the tree and slipped the handle of the bucket over a limb. Then he tied one end of the rope to the side of the handle and let the other end dangle down.

Ricky grabbed the rope and tied it to the lid of the box.

"That ought to do the trick," Pete said when they had finished. "Hurry, I hear someone coming. Let's hide."

The boys ducked behind a big bush as two other boys raced into the yard. They were Joey and Will Wilson.

"Say, Will, I thought sure I saw Pete and Ricky Hollister walking toward my house."

"They wouldn't come here," Will said. "They're afraid of you!"

"Well," Joey said, throwing out his chest, "I guess they are. Hey, look, what's this?"

The bully spied the box hanging from the string, but he did not see the bucket concealed in the leaves.

"It looks like a box full of money, maybe," Will Wilson said. "Let's open it."

"Don't you touch it. It's in my yard and belongs to me," Joey said.

The bully grabbed the box, giving the rope a hard jerk. He jumped back in fright as the donkey's head popped out and went *"Ee-aw! Ee-aw!"* At the same instant the rope tilted the bucket. Down came the water!

"Ow! Help!" they cried as the cold water soaked them.

"Who did that?" Joey said, glaring and looking around the yard.

Pete and Ricky, peeking through the bushes, choked down their laughter.

"Maybe the Hollisters did it," Will suggested, wiping the water from his eyes.

"How could they?" Joey retorted. "They're busy running that old merry-go-round of theirs." Then he added, "Hey, Will, you were here a while ago. Maybe you did it."

"Me?" his friend retorted. "Don't blame me. I got wet, too, didn't I?"

"Yeah, but you made *me* open the box."

"I did not," Will shouted. "You were the nosy one."

"You blame me for everything," Joey said, his voice rising. "You're not so smart. You're the one who wanted to fool the Hollisters by hiding the plane that day."

"I did not!" came the retort. "Who towed the old pontoon plane into the cove?"

"Yeah, but who almost got caught! A fine friend, you are," Joey said. "For two cents I'd punch you in the nose."

"Try it," Will said, thrusting out his chin, which was a bad thing to do, because Joey hit him with all his might.

Will staggered backward, sitting hard on the grass. Then he jumped up and the two boys started a free-for-all. Finally, Joey chased Will out of the yard. He himself went in the house.

"Come on," Pete said to his brother. "Now's our chance to get our bucket and the donkey box."

Pete put the box under his arm as Ricky shinned up for the pail and the two boys hurried off along the back street. On the way home, Pete remarked, "So it was Joey and Will who took the plane. I'm glad that mystery's cleared up."

"It sure is," Ricky agreed. Then he said, "Oh, Pete, look at that sign over there."

Posted on a telegraph pole was a colorful advertisement of the Jumbo Carnival.

"There's another one down the street on that billboard," Pete said.

As the boys walked home it seemed as if the

133

Jumbo Carnival advertisements were tacked up on all the streets.

Pete was worried. "Maybe they'll get people so interested they won't come to our school fair."

When the boys reached home Ann Hunter reported that ticket sales had fallen off.

"I know why," Pete said, and told about the signs they had seen.

"Well," said Ricky, "that's not going to stop me from building my racer."

He went for Gramp to help him and they hurried to the cellar.

"There!" Ricky said, after tacking a strip of chrome onto the body. "That's keen!"

"Your car certainly looks as if it has a lot of get-up-and-go!" Gramp said. "When are we going to try it out?"

Ricky turned the steering wheel admiringly. "How about tomorrow, Gramp? Could we take it out on Logan's Hill?" Logan's Hill was seldom used by cars.

"Fine," his grandfather said. "We can put your racer in the back of the station wagon."

"I'll tell the other kids about it, Gramp," Ricky said enthusiastically.

The next afternoon the elderly man was waiting for his grandson. "Hop in," he said, as Ricky ran up to the station wagon.

Ricky glanced into the rear of the car. How gleaming his soap-box racer looked, ready for its first test!

Ricky skidded wildly.

"Some of the other kids will be at Logan's Hill," Ricky reported. "Maybe we can race."

When they arrived, no one else was in sight, but ten minutes later three boys appeared with their soap-box cars.

"There's enough here for one heat," Gramp said, grinning. "How about you young lead-foots racing your crates down the hill together?"

Ricky was amazed and proud that Gramp knew so many racing words.

"Hurray!" the kids shouted. "Let's go!"

Gramp made sure that the contestants were in a straight line across the road. Then he shouted, "One —two—three—go!"

The cars started slowly, then gained speed as they headed down the hill. Ricky surged out in front by a few feet. Then another car took the lead for a short way.

Ricky was gaining when suddenly he saw a stone in the road ahead of him. He swerved to avoid it but too late.

The car hit the stone and Ricky skidded wildly to the side of the road toward a tree!

CHAPTER 14

Missing Machinery

RICKY'S soap-box racer came to a jolting stop against the tree. Ricky, stunned, had slumped over the wheel.

Gramp was the first to reach him. "Ricky! Ricky!" he shouted, pulling his grandson from behind the steering wheel.

The lad tried to get to his feet but collapsed onto the ground. "I—I can't stand up!" he said weakly. "Something's wrong with my right leg, Gramp."

"I'll take you to Dr. Gregory," his grandfather said, lifting him up.

By this time the other boys had finished the trial race down the hill. Now they hurried back to see what had happened to their friend. Worried, they followed Gramp to the station wagon where he gently laid Ricky on the front seat.

"Will you fellows bring Rick's racer back to our house?" he asked before starting off. The boys said they would.

After whizzing along the road to Shoreham, Gramp Hollister pulled up in front of Dr. Gregory's office and carried Ricky inside.

"I—I think my leg's broken," Ricky groaned as he

was placed on a cot. After being told what had happened, the physician examined the boy. All the while Ricky's leg throbbed with pain, but he gritted his teeth bravely.

"I have good news for you," Dr. Gregory said finally. "The leg is not broken. However, it is badly strained. I'll strap it, but you must stay home from school and rest for several days. By then it should be much better."

"Will I be able to ride in the derby?" Ricky asked fearfully.

"Perhaps," the doctor said, smiling, "but I can't promise that."

In the days that followed, Ricky was the center of attention as he lay in bed at home. His mother gave him ice cream for dessert whenever he wanted it. And Pam brought his schoolwork home and helped him with it every evening. Finally Ricky was able to get up and limp around his room with the aid of a cane.

All this time he worried about his racer. It had been brought home, and secretly Gramp Hollister and Dave Mead had repaired the damage. The first evening Ricky came downstairs, he saw it in the living room.

"It's all ready for you!" Gramp grinned.

"Oh, golly, thanks!" the boy cried.

As time for the school fair drew closer, Pete and his father made plans for erecting the large merry-go-round.

"Let's make a father-and-son project out of this,"

"I think my leg's broken," Ricky groaned.

Pete suggested. "We'll need a lot of other boys and their dads, too."

"Perhaps our local firemen will lend a hand. They're very clever at putting things together," Mr. Hollister said.

Pete went to see the fire chief, who agreed to lend six of his men the following Monday night. In addition, several boys from school and their fathers said they would be on hand at the Board of Education garage to help set up the big merry-go-round.

Monday night found the garage swarming with eager workers in overalls, among them, Dave Mead and his father, Mr. Hollister and Gramp.

"Where do we start?" Dave asked Pete, who was looking at the chart Mr. De Marco had given him.

Pete said, "First we unload."

A spotlight from a small fire truck was turned on the area so the workers could see what they were doing. The various parts of the merry-go-round were lifted off the truck and assembled in a corner of the schoolyard.

"Crickets, this is fun!" Pete said.

Upright steel poles were bolted into place and finally the wooden animals were set on the merry-go-round platform.

Pete and Dave made frequent trips to the garage, bringing out the gears that made the merry-go-round run. On their last trip the boys were startled to find Joey Brill standing alongside the big truck.

"Did you come over to help?" Pete asked him.

"No," the boy answered. "I just want to watch you guys put this thing together wrong."

"That's where we're going to fool you," Dave said. "We're doing it right."

The bully laughed loudly and replied, "We'll see about that," and hurried off.

By ten o'clock that evening the merry-go-round was ready for its first test. Everybody watched as Mr. Hollister, standing in the center of the carrousel, started the motor.

"There she goes!" Pete shouted gleefully as the calliope tooted and the merry-go-round began to revolve.

But suddenly it stopped and the organ made a weird gasping noise.

"What's the matter?" Pete called out.

140

"We'll have to find out," Mr. Hollister said, calling to the firemen. "Something must be wrong with the machinery."

After the men had made a quick examination, one of the firemen said, "A small gear is missing. That's why the merry-go-round stopped."

"How big is the gear?" Pete asked. "Maybe it's still in the garage."

The fireman said it was only about as large as a boy's hand but was very important. Pete and Dave dashed back to search the truck. They could not find the small gear.

"Well," Mr. Hollister said, "we won't be able to use the merry-go-round unless we find the missing gear or have another made."

"I wonder if Joey had anything to do with it," Pete said suspiciously as he and his father went home. "He was hanging around the truck and might have put the gear in his pocket."

"I would advise that you make a thorough search before accusing him," Mr. Hollister said.

After school the next day Pete organized a search party of boys and girls. They covered every inch of the garage and the schoolyard, but still the missing gear did not turn up.

At four o'clock Pam said she must leave. "I'm taking Holly and Sue to the nursery. We are going to fix costumes for the children there to wear to the fair."

"Okay," Pete said. "See you later."

"Crickets, this is fun!" Pete said.

When the three Hollister girls arrived at the nursery they were surprised to see that Mrs. Byrd, the twins' mother, was there.

"Did you have a nice time?" Pam asked her.

Mrs. Byrd shook her head sadly. "I traveled a long way looking for my brother-in-law," she said. "But I didn't find him. Then Mrs. Griffith said he was right here in Shoreham. I went to see him but Zack Byrd told me he would not help support the twins. I don't know what I'm going to do."

Pam was touched. "Perhaps now you'd like me to ask my father about a job. You might even work at *The Trading Post*, Mrs. Byrd. Shall I call him?"

"Oh, please do."

Pam went to the phone and soon was explaining Mrs. Byrd's problem to her father.

"I'd be glad to give her a temporary job in the office," Mr. Hollister replied.

When Pam told Mrs. Byrd the good news the woman was overjoyed. "You're the kindest people I've ever met!" she exclaimed.

"Dad says you may start tomorrow morning," the girl told her.

Pam and her sisters now went to help Mrs. Griffith, who had been making animal costumes for her nursery children to wear at the fair.

"Oh, how 'citing!" exclaimed Sue, looking at the various poodle dogs, roosters, pussycats, and rabbit costumes. "May I try one on?"

"Of course, dear," Mrs. Griffith said.

143

Sue selected two pieces and quickly got into them. Everyone laughed. Sue had on a rooster's head and a poodle dog's body!

She pranced around the room, then did a somersault. This made everybody laugh even harder. Then the group settled down to work.

Meanwhile, back in the schoolyard, Pete and his friends were just about to give up the search for the missing merry-go-round gear. "Maybe Joey hid it in his tree house," Ricky suggested.

The bully and several of his friends had a hideaway located in a tree surrounded by a thicket near Will Wilson's home.

"Let's find out," Pete said, and the three boys hurried off.

She pranced around the room.

Looking up to the tree house, Dave said, "Nobody's there now. We can search it."

They climbed rapidly up the rungs nailed to the trunk and stood on the triangular platform. Dave glanced up among the branches.

"Hey, fellows, I think I see it!" he shouted.

Near a crotch of a small branch a gear was tied to the tree trunk with rope.

"I'll bet that's ours," Pete said as he shinned up and untied the gear. He stuffed it into his pocket, then all the boys dropped to the ground.

They were just about to race off when Joey and four other boys rushed up. "Tryin' to raid our fort, eh?" Joey cried.

The five boys jumped on Pete, Ricky, and Dave. One big boy sat on Ricky while the others subdued Pete and Dave despite their gallant fight.

Joey yanked the gear from Pete's pocket and ran off with it as his four pals followed.

CHAPTER 15

Mischief

JOEY BRILL and his four friends scattered in all directions as Pete, Ricky, and Dave chased them.

"Follow Joey!" Pete cried out. "He's the one with the gear."

"Yikes, after 'em!" Ricky shouted, running, with a slight limp, behind the older boys.

But Joey had a head start and he was a fast runner. After a hot chase up one street, down another, and over several back-yard fences, Joey disappeared from sight.

"Fan out, fellows, and see if we can find him that way," Pete ordered.

Each boy took a separate street. After they had gone a quarter of a mile, Ricky suddenly spied Joey sitting on a curbstone, holding the gear in his hands.

The younger Hollister yelled for Dave and his brother, but by this time they were far away. Bravely,

147

Ricky took up the chase himself, crying out, "Pete, Dave, there he is! Help me catch him!"

Fearing that help for Ricky would soon be on its way, Joey raced off once more. The redhead lost sight of him when he turned the corner of the street where the day nursery was located. Finally Ricky had to give up because his leg hurt.

Halfway home he met his brother and Dave. All three boys looked glum as they discussed their chase.

"I guess you were the last one to see Joey," Dave said to Ricky. "Too bad we weren't with you to nab him. Now we'll need to have a new gear made for the merry-go-round and that may take a long time."

"Crickets!" Pete said. "Our fair is only a few days off!"

Nearing the Hollisters' house, the boys saw Pam, Holly, and Sue approaching from the other direction. Sue was rolling something along on the sidewalk, guiding it from one side to the other with a little stick.

"That's an awful tiny hoop Sue's playing with," Ricky said.

"It's big enough for a little girl," Dave said jokingly.

As the children came closer the boys could see that it was not a hoop at all that Sue was rolling. It looked like the missing gear!

Pete rushed up to look at it.

"Don't take my toy!" Sue pleaded as her brother examined the metal object. "I found it and I want to play with it."

"That's a funny hoop!" Ricky said.

"Just a minute," her brother said, turning the gear over in his hands.

"Jiminy!" Dave blurted out. "This is the thing we've been looking for. Where'd you find this, Sue?"

"In the back yard of the nursery," came the reply. "I was playing there with Jack and Jill when somebody ran by and threw this over the fence. I like the clickety noise it makes when I roll it."

"What luck!" Ricky explained, then burst out laughing. "If Joey had known any Hollister kids were around, he never would have thrown it there."

The boys quickly explained to Sue what they were talking about and she willingly gave up the gear. "I found something 'portant, didn't I?" she said, clapping her hands together.

"You're a little heroine for finding it," Pete said,

patting his sister's head. "We'll exchange it for another hoop you can roll."

The children trooped into the yard and Pete knocked a hoop off an old barrel stored in the cellar and gave it to his little sister.

"You can either roll this or make Zip jump through it, like a circus dog," Pete said.

He whistled and the collie came bounding toward him. When the boy held up the hoop, Zip leaped through it gracefully. "Now you try to make him do it, Sue."

Zip liked this and was still bounding through the hoop when Mr. Hollister arrived home. Pete and Ricky rushed to tell him the good news about the gear.

"Let's fit it into the machine tonight, Dad," Pete said.

Mr. Hollister agreed and directly after supper the Hollister men and boys went to the school grounds. The missing gear was inserted.

"Let's start the machine again and see how it works," Pete suggested.

"Okay, everything's ready," said one of the firemen, putting down his wrench.

The motor was put in operation and the boy pressed the carrousel's starting button. It began to turn and the calliope played exciting music. This time the merry-go-round did not stop. Pete and Ricky cheered and the firemen congratulated the Hollisters.

"Now we're all set for the school fair!" Ricky said.

"Not quite," his brother corrected him. "We have lots to do before opening night."

"What's next?" Mr. Hollister asked.

"The booths," Pete replied. "We erect them tomorrow night. The firemen who will be off duty offered to help us build them."

The next evening was clear and windless—a perfect night to build and decorate the booths. Amid the smell of fresh wood and the sound of hammers and saws, ten booths were quickly erected by the men and boys.

Then a committee of girls arrived to decorate the finished booths. They wrapped red, white, and blue crepe paper around the upright posts and along the tops of the booths, giving everything a very festive look.

"I just can't wait for the fair to begin," Ricky said, "and race my soap-box car."

His leg still hurt a little, but he was strong enough to drive his small car in the big event.

Shortly after nine, as everybody finished work on the booths, the firemen switched off the big spotlight on their truck.

"Good night!" "Thanks for your help!" The children and grownups called to one another as they started homeward.

"Won't Mr. Russell be surprised when he sees those pretty booths tomorrow morning?" Pam said as they entered their home.

The next morning the pupils of Lincoln School

came early to look at the gay booths in the schoolyard. But when they arrived, the children gasped in shocked amazement.

Every one of the little structures had been torn down!

The wood and the bunting lay splintered and tattered all over the ground.

"Oh!" Holly wailed. "How awful!"

"Who could have done such a thing?" Pam cried.

"The same people who have been trying to wreck our fair!" Pete exclaimed angrily.

"Right!" Ricky spoke up. "I'll bet it was Joey, or maybe Mr. Byrd."

"We're going to find out," Pete said grimly. "As soon as the bell rings, I'm going into the office to telephone Officer Cal."

Ten minutes after Pete phoned, the policeman arrived. Officer Cal was very angry when he saw the broken booths. Grim-faced, he asked the school principal about clues, but Mr. Russell knew of none.

The policeman examined the wreckage carefully, but could find no indication of who had caused the malicious damage.

"What a terrible waste!" Mr. Russell exclaimed. "Now we shall have to rebuild all the booths. I hope the guilty person will be found quickly and severely punished!"

"We'll find him," Officer Cal promised. "The law will catch up with him sooner or later." Meanwhile, things were happier at the Hollister home, where Sue

"Who did this?" Pam cried.

was sitting on her grandmother's lap listening to a story. She never tired of asking Gram Hollister about things that happened when Gram was a little girl.

"Now tell me about the olden times," Sue began.

This time Gram told about a white pony which she used to ride to school. She said that one day the pony poked his head into the school window and nuzzled the teacher, who was standing up reading to the children. The teacher was so frightened that she dropped her book, which landed on Gram's desk, making the inkwell splash and covering Gram's pretty dress with blue spots.

"Oh!" Sue said, giggling. "What happened then?"

Gram adjusted her glasses and remarked that she needed a polka-dot dress anyhow. Then someone gave the white horse an apple and he waited patiently outside until school was over.

"Like Mary's little lamb," Sue stated, and asked for another story.

But Gram said she had some mending to do and suggested that Sue play by herself.

"I know what," the little girl said as she wandered off. "Why don't I play with some of the rag dolls made for the fair?"

She went to the big carton in the hall. Inside were several gaily decorated dolls. Sue reached in and took out four.

"I'll take them for a walk," she told herself.

She put on her jacket and, clutching the rag dolls in her arms, went out to the back porch. When she saw Zip, Sue decided against walking and thought she would play house.

"You be the father and I'll be the mother," she said, wagging her fingers at the collie. "And these are four of our children."

Zip seemed to know what his little mistress meant and did everything she asked him.

"First we'll give them a pickaback ride," Sue said.

She put the four rag dolls in a row on the dog's back. Then, holding them up so they would not fall off, she followed Zip in circles around the yard.

"You've had enough rides," the little girl finally told her dolls. "Now it's time for you to take your naps."

She laid them in a row on the porch and covered

"Help! Help!" Sue shrieked.

them with a little blanket which she kept in her doll carriage.

"Now, Zip," Sue remarked, "we'll have to sit right here with these babies until they finish their naps."

Just then a big black dog and a small white one appeared out of the bushes on the edge of the Hollisters' property. They looked at Zip but did not advance a step farther.

"You can go ahead and play with them until I call you, Zip," Sue told her pet.

The three animals began to frisk around the yard, chasing each other and nipping playfully at one another's tails. While they were frisking, Sue went into the house to get a drink of milk and a cookie.

As the dogs raced around the back porch, the black one suddenly stopped and looked at the dolls. Approaching them, he sniffed, then took one in his teeth and carried it off. The white dog did the same.

Zip looked on bewildered for a few moments, not knowing what to do. Then he went over and gently nudged his two pals as if to say, "Put those dolls back where you found them."

But the two visiting pets had other ideas. They raced around the yard, shaking the toys in their teeth and ripping them.

Then the white dog dropped his rag doll and tried to get the one out of the black fellow's mouth. What a mad scramble as the dogs rolled over and over!

The poor doll came apart, its stuffing scattered over the yard. Now the dogs went back to take the remaining two. They hopped onto the porch and grabbed the dolls in their teeth just as Sue opened the door.

As they started to shake the dolls vigorously, Sue saw the wreckage and shrieked, "Help! Help!"

CHAPTER 16

Owl Signals

HEARING Sue cry out for help, Zip knew what to do. First he bounded over to the black dog and tried to grab the rag doll from the animal's jaws. When the black dog would not let go, Zip gave him a little nip. Frightened, the black dog yelped, dropped the doll, and ran out the yard.

The collie then turned on the white dog. In a couple of minutes he made him give up the doll and chased him off.

The cloth toys which Gram and the girls had made

159

for the fair lay in shreds on the ground. Sue, in tears, ran over to pick up the remains as Pete and Dave Mead, who had come home for lunch, hurried out to see what the commotion was about.

Between sobs, Sue told them what had happened. Pete patted Zip on the head. "Good boy to protect the dolls," he said. "You're a dog hero."

"But look at them now!" Sue wailed, clutching the chewed-up remnants of the toys. "Pam can't sell these at the school fair and it's all my fault for taking them."

Pete said he thought Gram surely would help make new ones, so the little girl hurried inside the house to ask her.

"Of course," Gram said kindly. "You and I will make four brand-new rag dolls."

Sue dried her tears and smiled. "Let's make a puppy-dog rag doll for Zip to play with," she said, " 'cause he's a dog hero!"

Gram and Mrs. Hollister laughed and said this was a wonderful idea. Sue's mother brought out an old nylon raincoat which had been discarded.

"This should do for Zip's rag puppy," she said. "It won't tear so easily when he plays with it."

Soon the rag puppy was sewed and stuffed. Sue ran for her crayons and drew eyes, nose, and mouth. The toy had a cute face.

"Zip will love you," she said, holding it up. The little girl hurried outside and gave Zip his reward. The collie sniffed and growled at it playfully. Then finally he took the rag puppy in his teeth and tossed it into the air.

"See!" Sue said to Pete. "Zip knows how to play with his toy already."

In a few minutes Sue went back to help her grandmother, who was now stuffing the new dolls. Pam came in and Sue told her about the accident.

"But Gram and I are fixing new dollies. Pam, don't you think it would be nice to make these into prize dollies?"

"What do you have in mind, dear?" Pam asked her.

Sue sat on a hassock, her chin cupped in her chubby hands as she thought. "I know," she said. "Let's make one blue eye and one brown. The girls who get these dollies can have a free ride on the merry-go-round."

"Why, that's super!" Pam exclaimed. "We'll put up a sign and it'll help sell the dolls. I'll have merry-go-round tickets handy."

When the four dolls were stuffed, Gram got some brown and some dark blue yarn and made the eyes.

"A person would hardly notice this at first glance," she said.

During the next few days, excitement rose high in Lincoln School. Soap-box racers of all kinds and descriptions could be seen in the schoolyard as the boys tested them out for the big race.

By this time Ricky's limp had vanished entirely

and he was in good condition for the event. His racer, too, was in fine shape for the derby.

One morning when Pete and Dave Mead reached school together they met Mr. Logan, the janitor, who looked worried. Everyone liked him and Pete wondered what the trouble was.

"Anything wrong?" he asked.

"Yes, there is. My brother's been guarding the grounds here at night, but the place is too big for one person. Some scallawag's been coming around tampering with the booths."

Pete looked at Dave. "Maybe we can help. What say?"

"Sure, Pete."

The boys went directly to Principal Russell's office and put the question to him. "It's a good idea," he said, "but you'll have to get your parents' consent. Bring written requests back with you this noon."

"Yes, sir, and thank you," the boys said.

Mr. Russell smiled. "Be sure to nab the intruder."

"We will," they promised. On the way to the yard to wait for the bell, Pete said, "Crickets, Dave, this will give us a chance to play real detectives!"

Both boys received permission from their parents to do guard duty. They could hardly wait for evening to come. Just before dark the two friends met Mr. Logan's brother in the playground. He was a tall, slender, gray-haired man with stooped shoulders.

"Well, have you boys any suggestions about how

Pete waited anxiously in the sandbox.

the three of us should guard the booths tonight?"

"I think we shouldn't stay together," Pete replied. "Let's take up posts around the schoolyard."

"That's good," Dave said. "But we ought to have some way to signal each other."

"I have it!" Pete exclaimed, snapping his fingers. "How about hooting like an owl? There's a family of owls in that big tree in front of the school so the noise won't be unusual."

This was agreed upon. Then it was decided that Mr. Logan should stand guard in the shadow of a doorway back of the school. Pete would lie down in the children's sandbox on the far side of the schoolyard and Dave would hide inside one of the booths.

"But we mustn't jump anybody unless he starts doing some damage," Mr. Logan warned as they went to their lookouts.

By this time it had grown dark and the street lights winked on. The minutes ticked past slowly as Pete waited, flat on his stomach in the sandbox, his eyes peering over the edge. For an hour nothing happened, and Pete shifted his position every so often so as not to become cramped.

Suddenly there was the hoot of an owl. Pete jumped up and returned the hoot. Instantly a hoot came from the doorway. Another sounded from the booth.

"Which one saw something?" Pete thought

excitedly as he dashed toward Mr. Logan's post.

Dave came on the run also, but each of them seemed surprised because nothing had happened.

"Who gave the first hoot?" Pete asked.

"I didn't," Dave said.

"Nor I," said Mr. Logan.

Was it possible that someone else had overheard what signal was going to be used and was playing a trick on them? The three watchers searched but could find no one.

Finally Pete said, grinning, "It must have been one of the owls in that tree in front of the school."

"I never thought of that," Mr. Logan confessed. "We'd better change our signal to a whistle."

They quickly decided upon a low, mournful-sounding whistle and practiced it. Then the three returned to their hiding places.

After half an hour had gone by, Pete saw a mysterious car silently pull up to the curb in front of the school. He warned the others by giving the agreed-upon whistle.

Mr. Logan stepped from the doorway, flattened his body against the school wall, and inched forward in the shadows.

Meanwhile the intruder got out, hunched over, and approached the booths. Pete arose and crept forward slowly.

The stranger disappeared into one of the booths for a few seconds, then came out. He had not done

The intruder stopped a moment.

any damage. Puzzled, the others waited. The intruder headed back for his car. Presently he lighted a match and in its glare Pete could see his face plainly.

The man wore a goatee!

Instantly Pete dashed after him. But before the boy could reach the intruder, there was an explosion behind them.

Mr. Logan cried out, "Fire! A booth is on fire! It'll spread and burn up everything!"

CHAPTER 17

A Wonderful Fair

AT THE sound of the explosion and the cry of "fire," Pete stopped running and glanced back. Flames were shooting up in all directions from the large booth on the school fairgrounds.

"What to do now," Pete thought. Should he chase the man with the goatee who had planted a fire bomb or help keep the flames from spreading?

The boy made up his mind instantly. He would tell the police later about the man. Right now he must help put out the fire.

"I'll get an extinguisher!" shouted Mr. Logan, the guard, and dashed into the school building.

Pete raced to the sandbox. "Dave, let's dump sand on the fire!" he called.

Dave rushed over and the two boys grabbed pails. Scooping up sand in them, they threw shower after shower of it onto the smaller adjoining booths which had caught fire.

In a few moments Mr. Logan appeared, an extinguisher slung over his shoulder. Pete ran for it, hurried toward the fiercely burning booth, and sent a stream of foam onto the flames. They were quickly put out. Dave had continued throwing sand onto the other booths and soon all the sparks were extinguished.

Pete sent a stream of foam onto the flames.

"Good work, boys," Mr. Logan praised them. "The whole place might have gone. Too bad we couldn't catch that firebug."

It was decided that the police should be notified at once and Mr. Logan went to phone them.

The boys surveyed the damage. "The big booth's in bad shape," Dave remarked angrily.

Pete looked it over and thought perhaps he and Dave with Mr. Logan's help could repair it. When the watchman returned, they got lumber and tools from the basement.

Presently Officer Cal arrived by car and heard a detailed description from Pete of the man who had set the fire. "Sounds like the goateed fellow we've been looking for all along," he said.

Pete nodded. The boy was surprised to learn from the officer that the suspected man, who they believed was connected with the carnival, had not been seen around the Jumbo outfit for several days.

"We're keeping a sharp lookout for him, though," Officer Cal said.

As he bade Mr. Logan and the boys good night, he told them that one of the town's police cars would patrol the schoolyard every few minutes to see if the intruder had returned.

After putting the burned booth in shape, Pete and Dave went home. Early the next morning Pete called police headquarters. He was told that the firebug had not been located yet.

Everything remained quiet in the festive-looking

schoolyard right up to opening time on Saturday afternoon. Then how gay and exciting everything became! The school band played and children milled about, some alone, some with parents.

Various games had been set up and the attractively decorated booths were full of things for sale. None looked more inviting than Pam's display of dolls. There were samples of five kinds from which to choose. The rest were wrapped in colored paper and tied with ribbon. On the booth hung a large sign:

WIN A PRIZE DOLL

When half of the dolls had been sold, Pam announced over the loud-speaker, "All girls having rag dolls with a brown and a blue eye will get a free ride on the large merry-go-round. Come to me for a ticket."

Immediately happy cries were heard from two girls who dashed up. How exciting it was to win a free ride on the carrousel!

Business became very brisk at Pam's booth. In a short time every doll, even the samples, was gone. When Mrs. Hollister came up with Sue, her oldest daughter's eyes were shining.

"Oh, we've made lots of money for the nursery," Pam cried excitedly.

"That's wonderful, dear," said her mother. "And now why don't you go around the fair and have some fun?"

"There's something else I'd rather do," Pam told

her. She leaned over and whispered into Mrs. Hollister's ear. Her mother looked surprised and Pam pleaded, "Please go with me. It won't take long."

"All right. Sue can stay with Gram."

The little girl was turned over to her grandmother, then Pam and Mrs. Hollister started toward the exit from the fairgrounds on their secret errand.

Just as they reached it, everyone there, including Ann Hunter, who was selling tickets, started to laugh. A car had pulled up and out of it came Jack and Jill and three other children from the day nursery with Mrs. Griffith. They were dressed like funny little clowns, gnomes, and animals. Jack was a rooster and Jill a poodle dog. They immediately began to cavort about among the crowd.

"This is as good as a circus!" exclaimed Ricky, who was munching on a piece of homemade taffy.

Just then an announcement came over the loudspeaker. "Now it's time for the first heat of the soap-box derby," the school principal said.

"We'd better wait and see it," Mrs. Hollister said to Pam.

"Oh yes."

Mr. Russell read off four names, including that of Ricky Hollister. "The first two will qualify for the final event," he continued.

The course was laid out on a steep street which ran into the school property. Ricky and the other three boys pushed their cars up the hill. When they were seated, Dave Mead and members of his committee held the cars in place so that the front wheels were even.

"One—two—three—go!" Mr. Russell called to the racers.

The cars were released and started to roll down the hill. Faster and faster they went!

"Come on, Ricky!" his brother and sisters shouted.

The soap-box cars zipped down the street with Ricky in second place. As they whizzed into the schoolyard, he nosed out the lead car. Holly was so excited that she danced up and down screaming, "My brother's winning!"

But as the racers approached the finish line, the right rear wheel of Ricky's car flew off! The axle made sparks as it dragged across the pavement. The Number Two car shot past and came in first. Ricky

The wheel flew off Ricky's car.

had been going so fast, however, that even on three wheels he came in second.

The missing wheel meanwhile had bounced among the spectators. Ricky hurried to retrieve it just as the announcer said, "Second place goes to Ricky Hollister, who qualifies for the final event."

Gramp, who had been watching the race, hurried over to his grandson and said, "We must fix that wheel right away, Ricky. I think a cotter pin came loose, but no damage has been done."

As the next two heats of the soap-box race were being run off, Ricky raced into the school and borrowed a hammer, pliers, and screwdriver. With his grandfather's help he quickly fixed the runaway wheel.

"That won't come off now," Gramp Hollister assured him. "Get in there and win!"

"All ready for the final race!" came the announcement.

Ricky and five other boys pushed their racing cars to the top of the hill. As the cars were held in their places, the principal announced that a large silver loving cup would be awarded to the winner.

"Good luck, Ricky!" shouted Mrs. Hollister as she waved to her son.

"Are you all ready?" said a voice on the loudspeaker. "Here we go!"

"They're off!" the onlookers cried.

CHAPTER 18

Carrousel Capture

WITH the crowd roaring encouragement to the six young drivers, the soap-box cars gained speed along the racecourse. Faster and faster they went!

"Wow! Look at that red car go!" Dave Mead cried.

Two boys pulled into the lead and Ricky was third.

His heart pounded as he kept his racer on a straight line. Then inch by inch Ricky's car started to gain. Now he was in second place!

"Ricky! Ricky!" screamed Holly, as he whizzed by his family lined up along the course. They seemed to him like a blur of many colors.

In a few moments Ricky was alongside the leader. What a din from the onlookers as the two cars raced wheel to wheel!

Sue, jumping up and down, screamed, "Hurry, Ricky! Hurry!"

The finish line seemed to come toward Ricky Hollister with a rush. Suddenly the race was over and he steered to the side line, not knowing whether he or the boy in the red car had won.

"It's a tie, a tie!" someone cried out.

The school principal started to walk forward with the trophy—a silver cup. Whose would it be?

Mr. Russell spoke into a microphone. First he praised all the contestants, then said, "The winner of the soap-box derby is Ricky Hollister!"

As everyone cheered, the whole Hollister family crowded around their hero. What hugs and kisses! Then the boy's friends slapped him on the back with shouts of "Atta boy, Rick!"

As Mr. Russell presented the silver cup, Holly piped up proudly, "That's my brother!" Ricky grinned.

In a few minutes the group broke up and Pam and her mother hurried off on their secret errand. Other people returned to the various booths, the games, and the merry-go-rounds.

Holly raced to the edge of the fairgrounds where Domingo and the donkey cart were tied to a tree. Two customers were waiting to buy tickets from Holly's helper, Donna Martin. A boy and a girl climbed into the cart. When they were seated, Holly took their tickets, untied the rope, and drove them around for a few minutes.

When the ride was over, she found Mrs. Griffith waiting with the five youngsters from the nursery, still wearing their funny costumes. "Hello, Jack! Hi, Jill!" Holly called, waving to her little friends. "You going to have a ride with Domingo?"

"Your gram and gramp bought us all tickets," Jack announced. "Please take us for a ride right away.

I just can't wait." He handed Holly the tickets.

She thought for a moment, then replied, "All right, but we can't all fit into the cart at once." She remembered the time when poor Domingo had been upended as too many people tried to ride at the same time. "Oh, I know," Holly suddenly decided. "Jack, suppose you ride on Domingo's back and hold him down while the others get into the cart."

"That'll be fun," said Jack.

The rooster boy scrambled onto the burro's back and called out, "Cock-a-doodle-doo!"

"Now," Holly said to poodle-dog Jill, as the others stepped into the cart and took seats, "will you drive?"

Jill took the driver's seat and jiggled the reins. "Giddap, Domingo!" she called, and they started off. When people standing around saw the rooster crying

"Giddap, Domingo!" Jill called.

"Cock-a-doodle-doo" astride the donkey, and the poodle dog driving, they rocked with laughter. Several people took pictures.

Over at the two merry-go-rounds everybody was having a gay time too. The smaller carrousel was in full swing. While Jeff Hunter took tickets, Ricky, on duty again, helped the smaller children onto the backs of the wooden animals. Gramp Hollister took care of the starts and stops, and the young riders squealed with delight as they spun round and round.

"Next time I want to ride on the lion," said one little boy as he hopped off a deer when the ride was over.

The large merry-go-round was even busier. "We're doing a wonderful business!" Pete exclaimed to Dave as he looked at the long line of youngsters waiting to buy tickets at a nearby booth.

"Step right this way for your ride!" a boy named Bert called out as Pete pulled a lever to stop the merry-go-round. As it slowed down, the riders hopped off and another group quickly scrambled for their places.

Dave Mead, who had been helping, was off duty for a while. He wandered around the grounds and finally came to the entrance booth where Ann Hunter had just put her sack of money on a shelf inside the booth.

As Dave approached, he saw a man slyly edging toward the booth. Then, as Ann turned her head for a moment, the fellow grabbed the sack of money,

"Stop thief!" Dave cried.

tucked it under his coat, and ducked into the crowd.

"Stop thief!" Dave cried out. The boy gave chase, threading his way through the throng of people. "Stop that man! He has our money! He's a thief!"

"What man?" several astounded bystanders called out.

"That one up there!" Dave pointed out the thief who was making his way toward the large merry-go-round. "Stop thief!" Dave screamed loudly.

Pete heard the cry above the music of the calliope and the roar of the merry-go-round's engine. He glanced around and saw a man hurrying toward the carrousel. The fellow's face looked vaguely familiar to the boy. Where had he seen him before?

Suddenly Pete recalled the drawings Uncle Russ had made of the two men who had called on the De Marcos in Crestwood. Now it dawned on him who the man was—Mr. Goatee! *But he had shaved off his beard!*

The man grabbed an upright post of the merry-go-round with one hand and swung himself aboard. The riders stared in amazement as the fellow pushed his way among them, trying to get to the opposite side so he could jump off and escape in the crowd.

"Stop!" cried Dave, who had run up. "Pete, slow down!"

But the Hollister boy had another idea. He would speed up the carrousel so Mr. Goatee could not get off!

He moved the lever another notch and the carrousel whirled at a furious clip. It went so fast that the thief did not dare to step off for fear of being thrown and injured.

Now everybody at the fair had encircled the merry-go-round, including a good-looking young man in a police uniform.

"Officer Cal!" Pete thought in relief.

"Stop the merry-go-round, Pete!" the officer ordered, taking a pair of handcuffs from his pocket. "We've got him now."

"You bet we have!" Gramp Hollister said, rubbing his hands together.

Pete promptly obeyed. As the carrousel slowed down, the thief hopped off and tried to get away but Officer Cal and Gramp nabbed him before he could take two steps.

"Tom Weel, you're under arrest!" Cal said, collaring the man. The policeman took the sack of money from him and handed it to Pete. Then snap snap, the handcuffs were on.

"Let me go! Let me go! I'm not Tom Weel," the man complained bitterly, "and that's my own money. Give it back!"

"You'll have a hard time proving that," replied the policeman. "Shaving off your beard didn't fool us."

Officer Cal searched the prisoner and found a wallet containing his driver's license. A quick glance through it proved that the suspect had been lying.

"You're Tom Weel, all right," Officer Cal said

sternly. "You'd better confess everything or it will go extra hard with you."

As the man hung his head, Ricky called out, "You're an old meanie! You tried to steal our big merry-go-round."

"But you didn't get away with it because we chased you at the motel," Pete added.

One accusation after another was heaped upon the prisoner, who by this time was shaking with fear.

"All right, I'll admit everything," he said finally. "The Jumbo Carnival needed a new merry-go-round but couldn't find any. You Hollisters beat us to the ones in Crestwood and I figured we had to get them."

Later, without his partner's knowledge, he admitted, he had tried to steal the large merry-go-round and later ruin the school fair to make people come to the Jumbo Carnival.

Upon learning that Joey Brill was unfriendly to the Hollisters, he had induced the boy to sabotage the large carrousel by running off with one of the gears. He even suggested where Joey should hide it.

"That trick nearly worked," Mr. Goatee said ruefully.

"But the meanest thing you did," Dave spoke up, "was to knock down our booths and try to burn them."

The prisoner looked ashamed. "Zack Byrd warned me not to do anything dishonest," he said. "I should have listened to him, but now it's too late."

Then Tom Weel explained that Mr. Byrd was

perfectly honest, although at times he was hard to get along with. It was he who had tried to buy the large merry-go-round from Mr. Hollister. Weel admitted that he and Mr. Byrd had broken up their partnership the day before. From now on, Jack and Jill's uncle would run the Jumbo Carnival alone.

When the confession was over, Officer Cal led the prisoner to a waiting police car.

Pete took the bag of money back to Ann Hunter at the ticket booth just as Pam and her mother came hurrying into the fairgrounds with Zack Byrd.

After Pete brought them up to date on what had happened, Pam said, "I have some wonderful news. Mr. Byrd is going to help Jack and Jill."

At this moment the twins ran up. Their uncle bent down and hugged them, saying he would buy their clothes and food from now on.

"Goody," Jill said. "Now mother won't have to work so hard."

"Indeed she won't," Zack Byrd said, smiling. "She can help me keep the books for the carnival now that Tom Weel is no longer with me." Then he turned to Mrs. Hollister, adding, "I'm very pleased that you and your daughter showed me my duty to these two wonderful children. And now, Jack and Jill, how about some candy and a ride on the merry-go-round?"

Mr. Byrd stayed with the children the rest of the afternoon. When the fair was about to close, a voice came over the loud-speaker.

"This is Pete Hollister speaking," it said. "Zack

Pete made a special announcement.

Byrd's Jumbo Carnival will be open tonight and everybody is urged to attend it."

A cheer went up from the people, then Pete said, "We haven't counted the money yet from our own fair, but it will be a large amount for the Shoreham Day Nursery."

While Pete was making his announcement, Mr. Hollister arrived at the school fair with Mrs. Byrd. She was overwhelmed to hear of her brother-in-law's decision and thanked him.

Jill Byrd, in her little poodle costume, looked up seriously. "Now," she said, "we can all be happy like the Happy Hollisters."